Sara's Summer

Sara's Summer

Naomi R. Stucky

HERALD PRESS
Waterloo, Ontario
Scottdale, Pennsylvania

Canadian Cataloguing-in-Publication Data
Stucky, Naomi R., 1922-
  Sara's summer

ISBN 0-8361-3534-2

1. Hutterite Brethren—Fiction.   I. Title.

PS8587.T833S37 1990   C813'.54   C90-094846-9
PR9199.3.S884S37 1990

The paper used in this publication is recycled and meets tl
minimum requirements of American National Standard for
Information Sciences—Permanence of Paper for Printed
Library Materials, ANSI Z39.48-1984.

SARA'S SUMMER
Copyright © 1990 by Herald Press, Waterloo, Ont. N2L 6H7
    Published simultaneously in the United States by Herald Press,
    Scottdale, Pa. 15683. All rights reserved.
Library of Congress Catalog Number: 90-71017
International Standard Book Number: 0-8361-3534-2
Printed in the United States of America
Cover art by Edwin Wallace
Design by Merrill R. Miller

*In memory of my beloved husband Solomon,
and for our granddaughters Moyo, Miriam, and Thea.*

1

The white bus with the blue-and-green stripe crept steadily northward. Sara stared at the driver's ruddy neck and broad shoulders. She felt bored, tired, and restless. The bus had left Toronto at six yesterday evening. Except for a brief stop in Sudbury, at eleven, it had been moving all night.

Sara had slept from time to time but didn't feel rested. Now she was hungry. But more than anything she missed her morning wake-up shower and grooming. She longed for her toothbrush, neatly packed in her bag nestled deep in the belly of the bus. Why hadn't she considered the journey's length and put the toothbrush in her purse?

Opening her purse, she took out a comb and small mirror. As she combed her hair, she studied her face. Her pale complexion contrasted with her dark eyes and hair. She had been told not to wear makeup when she met her relatives. But she wouldn't be seeing them until late tonight. So she applied a bit of blush to cheeks and lips. That felt better.

She stretched her legs and arms, one at a time, in the narrow space. She didn't want to waken the elderly woman who sat at her right. She was glad the woman was still asleep. Last night she had talked constantly. Her light snores, punctuated by occasional whistles, were annoying. But they disturbed Sara less than that constant boring chatter.

Sara moved her tongue gently over her teeth, trying to eliminate the furry feeling. Maybe if she thought of things outside herself she wouldn't notice her physical discomfort. She turned to the summer holidays just beginning. She was on her way to Manitoba to visit grandparents, uncles, aunts, and cousins she had never seen. The thought filled her with both curiosity and dread.

She knew little about them. Her father had told her he had left them years before she was born because they had "come to serious differences in very important matters." What these matters were he had never explained. Sara understood that she wasn't to pursue the subject. She was worried that her relatives might not like her. What would she do then?

Tears abruptly came. Her father had suddenly died last winter. Now she was going back to the world he had left when he was not much older than she.

"You do have a number of relatives in Manitoba," her high school guidance counselor had said. Sara couldn't tell if it was a question or statement.

"Yes, but I don't know them. We never visited."

"Perhaps it's time that you did."

"My father left when he was very young. He never told me much about them. I wouldn't know how to act . . . or what to say." Sara bit her lip to keep it from trembling.

"But they know about you and about your father's death," said the counselor, holding up a letter. "The school received this. It's from your uncle. He invites you to come spend your summer vacation with them." She paused. "If you like living there, you're invited to stay."

Sara knew she had no other choice. After her father's death, she had become a ward of Children's Aid and was placed in a group home. Although everyone in the home had been civil, she had never felt part of a loving family. She wanted to belong to a family again. But she had serious doubts about fitting in with her relatives.

She stared out the window so the other passengers wouldn't see her tears. She especially didn't want the young man, sitting across the aisle and two seats behind her, to notice. He had gotten on the bus in Toronto, too. Whenever Sara looked at him, he was smiling at her. She suspected he was watching even when she wasn't looking at him. She hoped before the trip was over she could get to know him. But she feared making the first move.

She watched the dark-green fir trees and huge boulders of volcanic rock rush past, hurrying to some spot from which she had just come. The bus was passing over the Shield, a land too rugged to be plowed, where the rocks had to be blasted to allow for the narrow winding highway.

Except for the passengers, Sara hadn't seen another person since last night. The few tiny logging and fishing settlements through which they had passed seemed deserted. For the past hour, since daybreak, the bus had passed no settlements, only miles and miles of trees.

Consulting her map, Sara decided they were in Lake Superior Provincial Park. In this desolate country, where would they find breakfast? Her hunger was hard to ignore.

Suddenly the bus entered a high point near the edge of Lake Superior. No trees blocked the view of the lake. Sara gasped. It spread out like an ocean. She had never seen the ocean but imagined it couldn't look any bigger.

She wasn't easily impressed by bodies of water, having lived beside Lake Ontario for many years. Once she had taken the elevator high up the CN tower with her father. He told her that on a clear day one could see Rochester, New York. She had looked hard but decided the day wasn't clear enough for that. She could see the shoreline along Saint Catherine and almost to Niagara Falls, which gave her the impression the lake did have limits.

She had seen lakes Michigan and Erie from the air several times while flying with her father. From high up the lakes looked small. But now all she could see was a limitless expanse of silvery blue stretching to meet an iron sky.

She recalled the last plane trip she had made with her father. It had started just one year before, after school had ended. He and his group were beginning a summer tour which was to start in Chicago and take them to the West Coast of the United States, then to Vancouver and Winnipeg. School having ended, Sara was able to accompany them.

She also thought about trips they had taken when she was small. Then they toured the country in a small bus. Sara loved traveling with five adults and lots of musical instruments and musicians. She found each campground, hotel, and auditorium exciting.

As a child, she wasn't confined only to school hours or summer trips. The group had been her teachers, helping her through the entire public school curriculum by correspondence. After she entered high school she realized all the travel had given her a better knowledge of geography, music, and people than many of her peers.

The bus slowed. The driver jarred her out of her reverie. "Wawa! Thirty-minute stop for breakfast."

2

Sara looked around as she got off the bus. She smiled, remembering a story her father had told her about his experience in Wawa. It was his first trip east. He had been hitchhiking from Manitoba and had to wait in Wawa four days for a ride. That was in the late sixties when many young people were exploring the country on foot. Someone had even written a song about being stranded here.

She followed the passengers as they filed into the small restaurant. She wondered where the young man was but didn't risk looking back. At the hot-drink machine she got chocolate. After picking up a plastic-wrapped Danish, she sat at a table with two women who seemed to be traveling together.

The women chatted while they ate, ignoring her. The chocolate was thin and tasteless. The Danish was stale. The young man was sitting at a seat at a nearby table. Sara pretended not to notice. Her behavior puzzled her. She wasn't bashful—so why was she acting coy? She finished breakfast, made a quick washroom stop, then got back on the bus.

Minutes later the young man got on with the other passengers. The woman who had been her traveling partner didn't appear, so the seat next to Sara remained empty. The young man stopped to talk with the bus driver. Then, instead of going to his seat, he stopped beside her.

"The driver says the woman who sat beside you ended her trip here." He paused. "He gave me permission to sit here. Do you mind?"

"Of course not," Sara answered, putting as much indifference into her voice as she could.

"My name is Jon Thiessen. I'm traveling as far as Steinbach, Manitoba." Because she didn't volunteer similar information, he asked, "Who are you and how far are you going?"

"Sara Hofer. I'm going to a farm west of Winnipeg."

Jon looked interested. "Hofer! Isn't that a Hutterite name?"

Sara nodded, trying to hide her surprise. Never before had anyone asked her this question.

"You don't look like a Hutterite," he concluded, after looking her over carefully.

"What do you mean?" She hoped she hadn't sounded too defensive. She wanted to continue the conversation. But she wasn't ready to undergo a personal examination about a past she herself didn't understand.

"For one thing, they all dress alike. That is, all the women and girls do. And they have a certain facial and body language which is . . . different. Sort of an innocence other women don't have." He looked at her, unable to tell what she was thinking. Maybe he had offended her.

"My people are Mennonites," he continued, hoping to ease the atmosphere. "There are lots of us in Manitoba. Lots of Hutterites, too. Mennonites and Hutterites get along well. Historically, they're distant cousins."

"How's that?" Sara asked, her interest aroused.

"Both groups belonged to the early Anabaptists."

"The Anabaptists?" Sara asked. "Who were they?"

"A sixteenth-century religious group. They originated in Switzerland during the Protestant Reformation."

Sara recalled a chapter in her history book on the Reformation. She didn't remember Anabaptists. Her own religious training had been lax. Perhaps she could learn something about her background. She apparently had a willing teacher. And they would be on the bus together all day.

"How were the Anabaptists different from other Reformers?" she asked.

"They baptized adults, never babies. They advocated pacifism. During the religious wars, they refused to take up arms. Instead they farmed and raised their families. Their enemies, and they had plenty of them, called them sarcastically *Die Stillen im Lande,'* or 'the quiet in the land.'

"They had to move from country to country as their enemies became more and more aggressive," he continued. "Finally in the 1870s many emigrated to North America. Now you can find both Mennonites and Hutterites in much of the United States and Canada."

Apparently Jon knew a great deal about the subject. Sara, on the other hand, knew nothing. It would be easy to keep him talking.

"What caused Mennonites and Hutterites to go separate ways?" she asked.

"Several things. But the main difference was that the Hutterites took literally the New Testament idea of living 'in community.' "

"Oh, I do know about that," Sara volunteered, proud of knowing this much. "Some Hutterite families live in a colony and share all material things—houses, land, farm implements, food. No single family owns any of this. It's all owned equally by the group."

"Yes, in that way they're different from the Mennonites, although there are lots of kinds of Mennonites, too. But that's another story.

"Which reminds me, How did you get separated from them? It's obvious you haven't been living as a Hutterite. What's the story?"

"My father left the colony when he was young and never returned. . . . He was killed in a plane crash last winter—" Sara paused and swallowed. "I don't remember my mother. She died when I was small. She wasn't a Hutterite

"I'm going to spend the summer with my father's family. I've never seen them."

"Your father must have felt deeply about whatever it was that made him leave the colony."

"He was a musician."

"That explains it. Hutterites don't believe in using musical instruments. And music was your father's life."

Sara nodded. "But enough about me and Hutterites. What about you?"

"I've just finished my second term at Guelph, studying grain agriculture. I'm particularly interested in the development of strains of grain sturdy enough to withstand both the dry western summers and rigorous winters. My father owns a large farm south of Steinbach."

"Do you always go home on the bus?" Sara was thinking about the enormous amount of time consumed making the trip.

"I like to go by bus this time of year. Northern Ontario is so beautiful, so scenic. It also gives me time to adjust my thinking from school life back to farm life. At Christmas I fly to save time."

Sara nodded. Flying would certainly be faster, but her uncle had sent a bus ticket. She realized that after having already traveled eight hundred miles in fifteen hours, she was still five hundred miles and at least ten hours from her destination. The distance was almost beyond understanding. She had to admit, however, that the past four hours had passed quickly.

They had talked constantly. He knew so much about the geography of northern Ontario, farming and land in general, the history of Mennonites and Hutterites. He had been so helpful, never seeming surprised or amused by questions she was afraid might sound stupid.

He hadn't asked more questions about her past. She appreciated his kindness and tact. She was beginning to like him a lot and was glad they would be together the whole day.

For the past hour the highway had skirted the shore of Lake Superior. Each time Sara was impressed by its vastness. It was past noon when they finally stopped for lunch in Thunder Bay.

They had an hour. Jon suggested they eat quickly, then exercise their legs by exploring. He led Sara up a rugged hill where they had a panoramic view of the huge port. Many cargo ships were at anchor.

"They're beginning to load the first grain from this year's harvest in middle America." His arm made a sweeping gesture toward the ships. "In a couple of months, they'll begin carrying grain from the Canadian prairies."

"Where is it all going?" Sara asked.

"To cities along the Great Lakes, where it will be processed into flour and cereals." He paused. "Some of it will travel up the St. Lawrence into the Atlantic Ocean, then on to European ports."

"There must be an awful lot of it." Sara felt the need to say something.

Jon nodded. "You've probably heard the expression that the middle of North America is the 'breadbasket of the world.' "

Sara had never heard it but didn't want to admit ignorance. She looked to see if Jon expected a response. Apparently not.

Jon was gazing at the longshoremen scurrying like a colony of industrious ants. Sara studied him in profile. He was quite good looking, she thought. Blond wavy hair, large, alert blue eyes, a well-shaped nose and chin. Standing beside him, she realized how tall he was. The top of her head came scarcely to his shoulder.

He turned and looked directly at her. Her face became hot. She felt it reddening. They laughed.

"Thunder Bay used to be two cities—Fort William and Port Arthur." He hoped by talking he could ease their mutual embarrassment. "The entire region was called the Lakehead."

"When did it get the name Thunder Bay?"

"Sometime in the late sixties, I think. I don't recall exactly." Jon chuckled. "My father told me that they voted on it and only a minority wanted the name, but they won by a devious method."

"What did they do?"

"Well, the story he told was that more people wanted to keep the name of the area, but they couldn't agree on whether to call it just Lakehead, or The Lakehead.

"So those who preferred Thunder Bay accommodated the other two groups by putting both names along with Thunder Bay on the ballot. Naturally, the two Lakehead names got well over sixty percent of the votes—but neither got as many as Thunder Bay did."

"Clever." Sara smiled. "I like Thunder Bay better."

"Yeah. Me too. But apparently many of the people who had lived here all their lives were disappointed."

Always mindful of time and fearful of missing the bus, Sara looked at her watch.

"We still have half an hour," Jon assured her.

"How do you know?" she asked in surprise. "You haven't checked the time."

"Well, am I right?"

"You are!" Sara looked directly at him. "Absolutely incredible!" she replied, shaking her head.

18

"Not really. When you grow up on a farm and spend most of your daylight hours outside without a watch, you get used to telling time by the sun and shadows."

He smiled. "Through experience you also get a certain feeling about how much you can accomplish in sixty minutes."

"Hey! Look over there." He pointed away from the port to a long, low island in the lake.

"What about it?" Sara asked, puzzled.

"What does it look like?" His voice hinted at mystery.

Sara studied the island. "Like a long, low rock, round at one end, and pointy at the other end."

"Use a little imagination. If the sun were setting behind it instead of shining directly above us, wouldn't the island look like a huge person, lying on his back?"

"I guess so," she conceded.

"Many people have thought so. It's called 'The Sleeping Giant.' The Indians had a legend about it, but I don't remember how it goes."

Sara was silent and a bit disappointed. She wished he had remembered the legend.

"We'd better get back to the bus." He took Sara's hand and led her down the steep steps.

3

The bus crept on and on all afternoon. Scenery had become a monotonous maze of scrub cedar and pink and gray boulders that seemed to push against the narrow two-lane highway. Sara felt as if she had entered an endless, long green tunnel. The monotony and lack of sleep had tired her.

Some of the passengers were asleep. Others spoke to their companions only infrequently. Jon had fallen asleep shortly after they had left Thunder Bay. Sara envied him. She tried to think of ways to break the monotony.

She searched for a glimpse of wildlife among the passing trees but saw only more trees. Suddenly the bus passed a sign, "Entering Central Time Zone." She moved her watch back an hour and sighed. Only three o'clock.

* * *

Sara swayed gently to the rhythm of the music. Five young adults were performing on stage. She watched her father bob his head and shoulders while strumming his guitar. Knowing the beat of the drums by heart, she prepared for each clash of the cymbals. The music stopped; the crowd roared.

Now the music was soft and sweet, like a lullaby. A woman cradled her in her arms, singing softly. Sara felt safe. The woman's long, golden hair tickled her cheek. She reached up and grasped it. It was fine and silky. . . .

* * *

Someone was tapping her arm. "Wake up, sleepyhead!"

Jon was smiling at her. The bus had stopped.

"We're in Dryden. Time for supper."

Sara consulted her watch. "Isn't it early?"

"Maybe, but the next town of any size is Kenora— and it's a hundred miles away. That would make supper late."

Most of the other passengers had left the bus. Jon took Sara's hand as she stepped down. She took a deep breath of the crisp, cool air, fragrant with northern Ontario pine.

"How long was I asleep?" she asked.

"I woke up at four and you were really sawing wood." Jon chuckled.

"Was I *actually* snoring?" she asked in horror.

"No. That's just an expression we use on the farm, living so close to the forests," he assured her. "You had such a peaceful expression on your face—like a little girl. Did you have a nice dream?"

"I guess so, but I don't really remember," she replied.

"We'd better get inside and order something. We have only forty-five minutes here."

They entered McDonald's and stood in line. As she waited, she remembered a funny habit of her father's. He would never play the fast-food naming games. At McDonald's he refused to put the *Mc-* before the various foods. At another chain he insisted on ordering the large, middle-sized, or small burger instead of the Papa, Mama, or Baby burger. So many pleasant memories. . . .

The lines moved slowly. Jon looked around, studying the other customers. Sara became restless. She realized Jon hadn't spoken to her for some time.

To get his attention, she asked, "Will we *ever* get out of trees so we can see more than a few feet in any direction?"

"Oh, yes. It will happen all of a sudden," Jon replied.

"When?" she pleaded.

"Just after we cross into Manitoba the trees will suddenly fall back. Then the prairie will spread out around us."

"How long until then?"

"About three hours. This time of year, the sun doesn't set until after nine. Then we have an hour of twilight. So you'll get to see it happen."

The line had moved. The clerk was waiting. After their order was filled they found a table in the nonsmoking section. Jon turned talkative again.

"The trees pull back like the opening of a curtain and the whole stage of prairie will appear in front and on both sides of us." His eyes were dreamy and his voice poetic.

Somehow Sara endured the next few hours, until Jon's prophecy came true. The dark green walls of pine receded abruptly. The lush moss green of the prairie surrounded them. Backing away gradually, the sun finally set, leaving a rich salmon-pink sky.

Jon could hardly contain his excitement as he looked at the fields he knew so well. He tapped his fingers constantly on the armrest between him and Sara. His behavior made Sara nervous. It reminded her of the unknown she was about to enter.

"How long before Winnipeg?" she asked.

"About two hours. But I'll be getting off at Steinbach, which will be in about an hour."

Sara felt sad that their pleasant acquaintance was about to end. So many questions rushed into her mind.

"Tell me more about the Hutterites. What can I expect? How should I act? I'm *so scared*," she confessed.

Jon looked into her face. He seemed to sense her fear was real. He took her hand and held it gently. "Don't be afraid. They don't know what to expect from you, either. They're probably afraid too."

"But there are so many of them—and just one of me!" she cried.

"But you're an outsider, coming in to their close-knit community. They may fear you'll cause problems for them."

"What problems could I cause?" She laughed nervously.

Jon smiled. "I've known you only a few hours, and I'm sure you won't cause any problems. But they don't know you yet. Only that your father didn't fit into their group.

"They might have reservations about you, too, based on their experience with him."

Sara thought about her gentle, soft-spoken father. She couldn't imagine his not getting along with anyone. She had often pondered his reluctance to talk about his past. If only he had told her more about his family. If only he had explained those irreconcilable differences.

"I'll explain when you're older. When you can understand" was all he'd ever say.

"Take it easy. Don't worry. Just go with the flow. Take one hour at a time," Jon said, seeing Sara's intensity.

"Tell me what I can expect," she pleaded. "I'm so afraid of saying and doing the wrong thing."

"First, remember they invited you. They want to get to know you. They'll be friendly. Hutterites are always friendly to outsiders if they know the outsiders genuinely want to learn about them and their ways. Like anyone else, though, they don't appreciate having their ways criticized."

"My father gave me the distinct impression their lives are limited, their ways extremely restrictive."

"That's true. They've followed the same practices for over four hundred years. Insisting on no change has given them stability and kept them together."

It didn't work for my father, Sara thought.

"When you think about problems our modern world faces, you have to admit their way has some advantages," Jon continued.

"You say, 'Go with the flow.' Exactly what do you mean?"

"Just be your own cautious, sensitive self."

Sara smiled. She remembered her earlier decision to "act cool," to let Jon make the first move. Throughout the day she had rarely spoken first.

She was, she realized, instinctively cautious and sensitive. Jon had realized it after a few hours. He had liked her. There was no reason her relatives shouldn't like her, too. Smiling at Jon, she squeezed his hand.

The bus was approaching Steinbach. Jon pointed out various farms and told Sara their owners' names.

"Those are all Mennonite names," he explained. "Most are my relatives."

Sara noted the names on passing mailboxes. "There seem to be a lot of Friesens."

Jon nodded. "If you went down this side road, you'd see a big sign on a barn, *Friesen Seed Farm.*

"When my Uncle Henry from Ontario first visited, he said, 'So that's where all the Friesens come from.' "

Sara smiled. Jon smiled back. "Not a good joke really, but one which lives on in my family."

They passed field after field of green wheat in the flat country. Suddenly, amidst all the green, a blue lake appeared.

"What a strange place for a lake!"

"It's not water," Jon explained. "It's a field of flax in bloom."

Sara was embarrassed.

"Lots of people have mistaken a field of flax for a lake," Jon assured her. "It gives that illusion."

The bus had entered Steinbach. Before it reached the station Jon saw his family's station wagon. "There's my dad, and my mom." He pointed to a handsome, portly, blond-haired, middle-aged couple standing by the bus station.

"The bus stops here for fifteen minutes. I'd like you to meet my folks," Jon said quickly.

They had to wait for other passengers to get off. Then Jon took Sara's hand, helped her off the bus, and led her to his parents.

"Mom, Dad, I want you to meet Sara Hofer. We rode together all the way from Wawa. Actually we both got on the bus in Toronto but didn't meet until Wawa." He paused, then gave his mother a hug.

Mr. Thiessen shook hands with Sara. "Did you have a good trip?" His eyes twinkled.

Sara noticed he spoke English with a German accent. "Yes, a good, *long* trip, but Jon kept it interesting," she said.

"So. My son, talking too much, like always." He shook hands with Jon and squeezed his shoulder affectionately.

Jon's mother shook Sara's hand. "Hofer. A Hutterite name, no?"

"Yes, Sara's going to spend the summer with her relatives west of Winnipeg. She has never seen them," Jon explained.

Mr. Thiessen nodded. "Which colony?"

Sara was at a loss. In his infrequent references to it, her father had called it just "the colony." What had her uncle called it in his letter to her school adviser? Then she remembered. "Gadenhof," she replied.

Mr. Thiessen looked first at Jon, then back to Sara, and smiled. "I think you mean *Gnadenhof*. In German a *hof* means an enclosed or private area. It could be a courtyard, a garden, maybe even a meadow. Gnadenhof could mean garden of grace or colony of grace."

He paused. "I'm surprised my talkative son didn't explain."

"The name of the colony didn't come up in our conversation," Jon replied, apologetically.

Sara realized now that Jon got his talkative nature from his father. From him Jon had learned so many little details about so many different things, and the pleasure of sharing them with others. She liked his parents and wished she had more time to learn to know them.

"All aboard! All aboard!" the bus driver called.

Jon's mother put her arm around Sara. "You must pay us a visit sometime."

Then Jon took Sara's hand for a last time and led her to the bus. He handed her a card from his pocket.

"This is my summer address here at home. My school address is on the back." He spoke quickly.

Taking it, Sara thought, *He must have written it this afternoon while I was asleep.* "Thank you." She looked into his eyes.

"Be sure and write and tell me what your summer's like." He paused. "If—no *when* you're back in Toronto this fall, be sure to let me know your address. I'll write, and come see you sometime. If you like."

"I'd like that very much. Thanks for everything." She gave his hand a squeeze.

Jon squeezed back. With his other hand, he touched her shoulder gently.

Sara turned and stepped into the bus. It moved out of the station immediately. Her eyes filled with tears as she waved until the Thiessen family was out of sight.

In just over an hour I'll be in Winnipeg, she thought. Would she be back in Toronto in the fall? Jon seemed to think so.

4

It was dark when the lights of Winnipeg came into view in the distance. They looked like the single strand of a pearl necklace, stretched taut across the vast prairie.

Once in the city, the bus continued to move for some minutes before stopping at the well-lighted station.

Sara remained in her seat, allowing the more impatient passengers to pass. She looked out the window and studied the people meeting the arrivals. She was searching for someone who had come to welcome her. She felt a slight panic as she considered the possibility that no one had come.

Then she saw them. A bearded man in his sixties, wearing thick glasses. And a younger one who looked much like her own father, except that he too wore a beard. They were staring at the descending passengers as if looking for someone.

Both men wore black felt hats and dark jackets and trousers of an unfamiliar style. She assumed they were her Hutterite relatives. Realizing they wouldn't recognize her, she promptly went to them.

"I'm Sara," she explained, extending her hand to the younger man. "You must be Uncle Joshua. You look a lot like my father."

"Yes, and this is your grandfather." Joshua shook Sara's hand warmly, then handed it to his father.

The old man took her hand and shook it warmly and long. Peering through his heavy glasses, he studied her face.

"Jonas's daughter. I see your father in your face. Come. We still have a long drive."

Sara's suitcase now stood alone on the platform where the bus driver had put it. "This must be yours," her uncle concluded, picking up the bag.

Sara followed them to a worn station wagon parked nearby. Her grandfather opened the back door for her and her uncle placed her bag on the seat beside her. Then the men took their places, her uncle driving.

Almost immediately the men began talking in German, ignoring Sara. Since she couldn't understand, she was left with her own thoughts. *They seem kind and friendly, but they don't like small talk. No questions about how my trip was or anything else.*

After leaving the city, the station wagon traveled west on the Trans-Canada highway. Sara wished she could see where they were going. But even in the soft darkness she could tell, from the vehicle's movements, that the land was flat and the road straight. Stars twinkled like diamonds in the black velvet sky.

An hour later, the station wagon left the highway. They were on a gravel road twisting through rolling country. Sara realized they hadn't passed through any towns since leaving Winnipeg. Occasionally they passed farms with lighted yards.

She wondered if Gnadenhof would have electricity. She remembered having heard or read somewhere that some religious groups didn't believe in modern conveniences such as electricity. She yearned to know more about the world she was about to enter.

The men had spoken only a few words to her since getting into the car. It would be best to watch and listen carefully, she thought. *I'll ask questions or do things only after I've thought it through.*

Slowing, the station wagon turned into a large farm with many buildings. Sara was relieved to see electric lights both outside and inside the houses.

Her grandfather turned and said, "We're home."

He got out of the car and opened her door. Her Uncle Joshua carried her suitcase along a long sidewalk, lined with flowers.

Neither man spoke until they reached one of the small white houses where a porch light was shining. Her grandfather said something in German to Joshua, then walked on.

Opening the door, Joshua motioned for Sara to enter. A woman met them. She was wearing a long, figured skirt. Above it was a blouse covered by a large, plain apron. On her head was an attractive blue polka-dotted kerchief tied under her chin. Except for the light blouse, all her clothing was dark.

"This is your Aunt Rebekah," Joshua said.

Rebekah gave Sara a gentle hug and kissed her cheek. "Welcome to our home. You will stay with us."

She looked at Joshua and spoke in German. He nodded and left the room, still carrying Sara's bag.

She turned to Sara and smiled. "You must be hungry. Would you like a glass of milk and a cookie before going to bed?"

"That would be nice," Sara replied.

"I will go to the kitchen and get it. Sit." Rebekah motioned to a small settee, then quickly left.

Sara sat down, her heart pounding. Had she said the right thing? To have refused the snack might have been rude. But by accepting it she had imposed on her aunt, who had to go to some other building for it.

She looked around the room. It was plainly furnished but neat. There were no pictures on the walls and only shades on the windows. There were several chairs besides the settee. The furniture was all homemade, the wood beautiful and highly polished. There was no clutter, no newspapers, clothes, or children's toys. A few books were stacked neatly on a shelf free of knicknacks.

The front door opened. Rebekah held a tray covered with a small white towel.

"We eat supper together at six," she explained. "But we can go to the kitchen for snacks." She set the tray on Sara's lap and removed the towel.

Sara looked at the tray. A little pitcher of milk, a glass, a small plate with a slice of thick white bread, a pat of butter, and a dab of jam. Two cookies and a knife lay beside the plate. Her mouth watered. She hadn't eaten since the light supper at McDonald's before six. Now it was near midnight.

She ate slowly, enjoying the freshness packed in every bite. The bread and cookies had been baked that very day, while she was riding the bus. She smiled secretly, comparing this food with her less-than-fresh breakfast and fast-food supper.

She looked at her aunt. "This is all absolutely delicious!" she smiled.

Rebekah looked up, nodded appreciatively, and smiled back. Then she looked down again at her hands, folded in her lap.

Sara studied her aunt's features, serene in repose. Her strange old-fashioned clothes, her carefully braided hair peeking from her kerchief, and her thick glasses made her look older than she probably was. Her smooth, clear skin made Sara think Rebekah must be younger than most of Sara's teachers or her classmates' mothers.

As soon as Sara finished eating, Rebekah motioned her to come upstairs. Passing through a small hall, they entered a dark room. The light shining from the hall allowed Sara to see that the room was small. It was furnished with two single beds and a chest of drawers. In one bed was a girl about Sara's age, who had just wakened. She sat, rubbing deep sleep from her eyes.

"This is your cousin Susannah. You will share the room."

She paused. "It is late. No talking tonight, girls," she added, softly but firmly.

She turned to leave the room, then turned again. "Susannah, you come down after the bell, like always.

33

Sara, tomorrow you can sleep late." Then she was gone.

"We eat breakfast at seven," Susannah whispered. "There are two bells, one at six-thirty to remind us we should already be up, and another fifteen minutes later to call us to breakfast." She turned away from Sara and further conversation.

Sara's body ached but her mind was wide awake. She noticed a towel and washcloth folded neatly on her pillow. She decided to wash. Opening her bag quietly, she took out a toothbrush, toothpaste, and nightgown. Tiptoeing to the door, she looked out.

Facing her directly across the hall were an open door and a sink. She picked up her things and crept to it, entered, and closed the door quietly.

The room had only the sink and a toilet. She would have liked a shower but could get along without one. Not wanting to wake the family, she turned the tap only halfway.

She enjoyed the feel of the warm soapy water as she washed. After brushing her teeth she felt like her old self. She slipped her nightgown on, picked up her things, and sneaked back to bed. The mattress was hard, the pillow soft—just as she liked them.

She closed her eyes and the past thirty hours rushed before her. She felt the movements of the bus.

Then she was on another bus. A much smaller one. She was sitting, strapped in a child's safety seat. Several other people were in the bus, too. They were laughing and singing, and there were lots of musical instruments and suitcases behind them. . . .

5

Sara opened her eyes. The sun was shining on her bed. She looked across the room. Susannah's bed was neatly made. There was no sign of her.

Susannah's dresses hung neatly from hangers on a rod under a high wall shelf. They had been pushed halfway to one side. Some empty hangers hung in the empty space. Several folded, dark kerchiefs with white polka dots were stacked neatly on the chest of drawers. With them were a comb and brush, some hairpins and a small pocket mirror. These, too, had been set to one side, leaving the other half of the chest top empty.

Sara concluded that the empty spaces were for her things. She unpacked her bag and hung her shirts and jeans on the empty hangers. After brushing and combing her hair, she neatly put her comb, brush, and hand mirror on her side of the chest.

In this room, too, there were no pictures on the walls, no large mirror over the chest, no curtains on the window. The shades were pulled half down.

Sara began to feel uneasy about her clothes. Her blue jeans and shirt would look out of place. So would her long, dark, flowing hair.

Should she borrow one of Susannah's dresses and stuff her hair under a kerchief? But she would feel ridiculous. For her, wearing their clothes would be like wearing a costume. And they might think she was making fun of them.

She decided to be herself and dress as she was used to. She wouldn't flaunt herself, though. So she chose her most loosely fitting jeans and shirt. She let the shirt hang outside, covering her hips. She tied her hair back with a rubber band and let it hang under the collar inside her shirt. If they wanted her to dress differently, she would cross that bridge when she came to it.

She went downstairs. The entire house seemed empty. She walked through the room where she had talked to Rebekah last night and eaten her snack. She stepped out on the porch which wasn't really a porch, only a large step. She couldn't see anyone—but could hear women singing in a building a short distance away. She walked toward the singing, on a sidewalk bordered with bright, multicolored flowers.

She noticed that all the buildings were of wood and painted white. Each was built in the shape of a rectangle with a straight roof. All appeared carefully arranged, equally distant from each other, around a square. The singing was coming from a larger building in the middle of the square.

She proceeded cautiously up the steps and hesitated in the doorway of a large kitchen occupied by several women preparing food. They hadn't seen her.

Rebekah stood at one table making meatballs. She faced a huge bowl half-full of ground beef. Beside the bowl were three huge pans filled with meatballs.

At another table two more women were shaping loaves of bread. Two more stood over a large double sink preparing vegetables. All were intent on their work, and all were singing.

Sara was fascinated. Never had she watched so much food being prepared at one time. Nor had she heard a group of women singing while they worked. Suddenly, noticing her, they stopped.

Rebekah came forward, smiled, and gave Sara a gentle hug. "Did you have a good rest?"

"Oh, yes," Sara replied.

"Come," Rebekah continued. "Meet your Grandmama and your other aunts." She led Sara to the oldest woman, who was molding a loaf of bread. "Your Grandmama. Her name is Sara, too."

The elder woman smiled and placed the loaf in a pan beside several others while peering at Sara through round spectacles. She wiped her hands on a towel, then pinched Sara's cheeks affectionately.

"You have your papa's eyes and hair," she said. Then she picked up another chunk of dough and began shaping it.

"This is your Aunt Rachel, your papa's oldest sister," Rebekah continued.

Rachel wiped her floured hands on her apron and

shook hands with Sara. "You have your papa's fine bones, his long, slender fingers, too." She continued to hold Sara's hand and look longingly at it.

"Over here," said Rebekah, leading Sara to the sink, "are your papa's other sister, your Aunt Mary; and his youngest brother's wife, Aunt Rhoda."

Mary and Rhoda each held up wet hands in apology. They nodded and smiled to show their pleasure in meeting her.

"Now for breakfast," Rebekah concluded. She led Sara into a huge dining hall which had long picnic tables with built-in benches along either side.

"You can sit here, now." She pointed to the end of the table and bench nearest the kitchen. "I will bring food." She disappeared into the kitchen.

Sara's head was swimming with this new information. Her name was the same as her grandmother's. Her father had never told her. She had four aunts who hadn't existed for her as recently as yesterday. She looked around the room. Would all this space be occupied by other relatives at mealtimes? She shook her head. It was more than she could take in at once.

Rebekah returned with a tray and proceeded to place its contents on the table in front of Sara: an orange, a bowl of prepared cereal, two slices of toast with butter and jam, and a small pitcher of milk. "We still have hot coffee. Would you like instead of milk?" she asked.

"Milk is fine." Sara looked at the small pitcher-ful, which was for the cereal. "If you have enough for drinking."

Rebekah nodded. She went back to the kitchen and

returned with a tall glass of milk.

The women in the kitchen began singing again. They were singing in German. Sara couldn't understand the words. She was puzzled, as she had been last night. She had studied German last year and thought she should be able to understand some of it. But this German sounded different.

She ate slowly, looking around occasionally to study the dining hall. The walls here, too, were bare except for a large motto with the words *All Things in Common* worked in cross-stitch embroidery. The tables, lacking tablecloths, were partly set. Salt and pepper shakers and a sugar bowl stood at several spots along the middle of each table. Knives, forks, and spoons had already been set for the next meal.

Two girls a little older than Sara entered. They pulled a double-decked cart stacked with plates, cups, and saucers which they began setting beside the cutlery. They chatted in that same unfamiliar German. Looking at Sara frequently, they smiled shyly, but didn't speak to her.

Like the women in the kitchen, the girls were wearing dark figured skirts falling to just above the ankle, white blouses, and plain dark aprons. Their hair was braided in the same unique style and covered with the blue polka-dot kerchiefs.

"I will take you to Susannah." Rebekah had entered and was motioning for Sara to follow.

Sara looked at her own dirty dishes. "Shall I take these into the kitchen?" She wanted to be helpful.

"Leave them in the little room between here and the kitchen. That is for washing dishes."

Sara carried her dishes into the little room and set them down beside one of the two large, deep sinks. Beside the second sink was a huge automatic dishwasher and beside it a spacious drainboard. Cupboards for dishes hung on all four walls.

She met Rebekah, who was waiting patiently for her outside the kitchen door.

They walked silently for several minutes. "What does Susannah do?" Sara asked politely.

"This week she helps in the kindergarten," Rebekah explained.

"What does she do there?"

"You will see."

Sara sensed a slight reprimand. Had she acted improperly? She had only wanted to carry on a friendly conversation. Apparently conversation for the sake of just talking wasn't encouraged. *Watch and listen carefully*, she thought. *Ask questions only when they invite you.*

Rebekah stopped. "Here."

They had come to a small, white building just outside the square. Sounds of little children playing greeted them. Rebekah opened the door.

A woman about Rebekah's age was sitting in a rocking chair, holding a child. Susannah and another girl about the same age were each occupied with a child. Several other children, their ages perhaps three through five, were amusing themselves with various homemade toys.

The women greeted each other and exchanged a few words in German. Sara heard her name mentioned. They were both smiling at her.

"This is your papa's cousin Anna," Rebekah explained. "That is her daughter Elizabeth."

She looked at the other girl and then at Susannah. "You girls make Sara comfortable. Show her how she can help."

Then Rebekah turned to Sara. "Susannah will bring you to lunch. You will sit at our table." With that she turned and left the building.

Sara smiled at her cousins and studied them briefly. They were both a little younger than she, and looked enough alike to be sisters. She wasn't sure if they really looked alike or if their identical clothes created that impression.

Their braided dark hair peeked out from under blue polka-dotted kerchiefs. Their full, dark figured skirts came almost to their ankles. They too wore white blouses. Their aprons were slightly lighter than those worn by the women. Both of them looked at Sara shyly but didn't speak.

"What can I do to help?" Sara asked, hoping to break the silence.

The two girls looked at each other as if expecting the other to speak first.

Finally Susannah spoke. "We keep the children contented and teach them to share." She paused. "Soon we will feed them."

Sara had hoped that when she saw Susannah again she would be more talkative than last night. It seemed that wasn't to be. Both girls returned to the small children they were attending.

Sara wasn't sure what she should do. Indecision was making her uncomfortable. She walked among the

41

children amusing themselves with the toys. They stared at her as if she were a freak. She smiled a lot and touched them gently, fearful of frightening them.

One of the littlest boys showed off his toy. Sara smiled broadly. "Nice," she exclaimed, holding out her hand to accept the toy. To her surprise, the child offered himself without releasing the toy.

Sara took his hand and led him to the remaining rocker. She helped him to her lap. Then she spoke to him softly as she gently rocked him. Anna looked at her and nodded approvingly. Sara smiled back, relieved to have been accepted by both the child and Anna.

The child lay quietly in Sara's arms for some time. Then he gave his toy to her, and with his hands free, reached up and timidly touched her hair. Several other children watched, then came forward to touch her hair, too.

She realized that the uncovered hair of an older person was a novelty to them. She bent forward and invited free and unlimited touching. She smiled and spoke to each child. When she felt they trusted her she touched them gently to show she liked them.

Promptly at eleven forty-five Rachel appeared carrying a large tray covered with a white towel. The children suddenly became more interested in Rachel than Sara.

Susannah and Elizabeth carried forward a homemade table with short legs and began setting it with old-fashioned tin plates and spoons. Sara gathered the little chairs scattered about the room and brought them to the table, placing one in front of each plate.

Each child seemed to have an assigned place. All slipped into their places without prompting and immediately bowed their heads. After Anna said a little prayer in German, both she and Rachel put large spoonfuls of food on each plate. Susannah filled glasses with milk, and Sara helped Elizabeth bring them to the table.

The adults stood quietly behind the children as they ate. Whenever a child began talking he was quietly shushed and told to eat. After they finished, the children were taken to the lavatory, where faces and hands were wiped clean.

Then they lined up at a small closet, where Elizabeth was handing a small rolled mat to each. In the meantime Anna and Rachel had cleared the table. Susannah and Sara moved it and the chairs to the edge of the room. The children laid down their mats, each at a previously designated spot, and promptly lay down.

"We go to lunch now," Susannah told Sara. The three girls left the kindergarten and walked silently toward the dining hall.

"When will Anna eat?" Sara asked.

"Rachel left food for her. She will eat alone while the children nap," Susannah explained.

Sara, realizing Elizabeth had said nothing to her, asked, "Will you eat with Susannah and me?"

"I must eat with my own family," Elizabeth replied simply. "We are at a different table."

Sara did not know what to say. She wondered if she had again overstepped bounds.

Susannah sensed Sara's discomfort and explained.

"We have assigned seats. The grandfathers and grandmothers still sit according to the old custom. The men at one table, women at another. Their children, our mamas and papas, sit by families."

Sara pondered this well-ordered society. "Where do the unmarried people sit?"

"Those who are in our parents' generation still sit with the grandfathers and grandmothers, all according to their age. Our grandmother sits at the head of the women's table. Our Aunt Mary, who hasn't married yet, sits at the foot."

Sara thought this order interesting. "When she marries, where will she and her husband sit?"

"Until they have children old enough to eat in the dining room, they will remain at separate tables."

Sara was intrigued by this obsessive fondness for order. "How old must you be to eat with the grownups?" she asked.

"Fifteen." Susannah and Elizabeth looked at each other.

"We started only a little while ago. Since our last birthdays." Elizabeth had finally spoken.

"Where did you eat before then?"

"There is a children's room on the other side of the kitchen," Susannah answered, a bit impatiently. "Enough talking!" she added, sounding more like her mother than a fifteen-year-old.

Susannah led the others into the quiet dining room already filled with silent adults. Elizabeth left them and quickly joined her family. Susannah took Sara's hand and led her to another table where her parents were. The three aunts Sara had met in the kitchen that morning, their husbands, and several other teen-age boys and girls were there, too.

After they were seated, Sara's grandfather said grace. Then everyone ate silently. Subdued voices made infrequent requests for the passing of some dish. Large serving dishes filled with plain, whole-some food had been placed at several strategic loca-tions on each table to make the passing efficient.

Suddenly Sara's grandfather tapped his spoon against his glass. All stopped eating and bowed their heads again. He recited another short prayer. Then all rose.

Sara was surprised and embarrassed. She had had time to eat only half the food on her plate. She want-ed to finish but realized everyone else was already leaving the table. *I'll have to eat faster!* she thought. She was glad breakfast had been late.

Susannah, Elizabeth, and the two older girls who had set the tables earlier stacked dishes on carts. Sara pitched in. The other two girls pushed the carts into the dishwashing area and Susannah motioned Sara to follow her outside.

After they left the hall Susannah turned and said, "We will go back to the kindergarten and watch the children while Anna and Elizabeth have their rest."

6

Anna and Elizabeth returned to the kindergarten an hour later. Then Sara and Susannah went back to their house.

"This is our private, quiet time. We can do whatever we wish, but we cannot leave the house," Susannah explained.

Neither girl felt like taking a nap, so Susannah crocheted and Sara wrote in her journal.

She had begun keeping a journal several years ago at her father's insistence. "Your life is different from the average girl's," he explained. "You should write about it so you remember."

Sara thought she'd remember her experiences without writing them. But she found she enjoyed writing, and the exercise was helpful in other ways. It improved her writing skills. And having to write something interesting every day made her watch people's behavior and ponder their motivations.

Her high school English essays always brought high marks. She recalled that her teachers frequently read hers to the class as an example of how other students should write.

It seemed every teacher told the class, "Look around you. You'll be surprised at all you'll see."

When other students complained that their lives weren't as interesting as Sara's, the teacher frequently replied, "That's because you haven't developed the power of observation. All people and experiences are interesting if you learn how to choose your subject and practice writing about it.

"Don't be afraid to write how you feel about your experiences. It might help you learn about yourself, and about what others feel."

Sara smiled. She would certainly have lots to write about when she returned to class this autumn. Or would she be returning? She had nearly two months to make up her mind.

She looked at Susannah, intently crocheting lace along the edge of a pillowcase. She had told Sara that she and Elizabeth wouldn't have to attend school, now that they were fifteen.

Sara was almost sixteen. If she stayed, *her* schooling would be over. Would she like that? No more assignments to be handed in next day. No more having to be in class when the weather was beautiful and she'd rather be outdoors. No more being stuck in school while her father was traveling.

She stopped. What made her think of that? There would be no more traveling with Father. That was why she was here this summer.

"Are you glad you don't have to go to school anymore?" she asked Susannah.

Susannah gave her a puzzled look. "I never thought about it. That is how it is here."

"What will you do?"

Susannah looked at Sara. "When?"

"In the future. With the rest of your life."

Susannah smiled. "There is always much to do here."

She paused. "I will stay here until I marry. Then I will move to my husband's colony."

Sara recalled that everyone she had met here was some sort of a cousin. Did these people marry cousins? Was that allowed?

She had to know. "Whom would you marry?"

Susannah shrugged. "Someone from another colony. I will know when the time comes."

"Aren't you people all related?" Sara hoped she wasn't being too nosy. She noticed Susannah was more willing to talk when they were alone in their room. She had to seize the moment to learn as much as possible. Especially since she would eventually have to decide whether to remain.

"We never marry first cousins. Our elders study our family charts. They can tell us who is allowed to marry and who is not."

Both girls were silent. Sara tried to take this in. Apparently everything in this culture had been thought out carefully. Members needed to make few decisions.

Finally Susannah spoke. "Aunt Mary will marry soon. I am crocheting these pillowcases for a gift."

After private hour, the girls put away their work and returned to the kindergarten. The mats were put away, and the children were playing happily.

The rest of the afternoon passed quickly. At five forty-five Rachel returned with food. The three girls set the table and helped the children settle into their places. After the children ate, the girls helped them wash and prepared them to be picked up by their mothers.

Sara recalled that the children were already in the kindergarten when she arrived in the forenoon.

"When did their mothers bring them?" she asked.

"Before breakfast. They stay here while their mothers work."

Sara had done a project for her Social Living class about the problems modern working mothers face finding adequate day care. She had collected articles describing the problem and legislative proposals to deal with it. These people seemed to have worked things out. She wished she had known about this system before reporting to the class.

The evening was warm. Sara sat on the porch step with Susannah and her mother. Rebekah held one of the three-year-olds from the nursery. Sara was surprised to learn that this child, whom they had watched all day, was Susannah's little brother. She had neither told Sara nor shown the child any partiality. The boy hadn't shown any preference for his big sister, either.

Sara learned there were two other brothers, ages seven and thirteen. During the day they had been playing around the grounds with the other children.

They ate their meals in the children's dining room each day, under the supervision of the German teacher.

During the summer these young Hutterites enjoyed the colony's most unstructured and unsupervised life. Having no regularly assigned tasks, they wandered in groups around the grounds, observing everyone else at work. They improvised their own playtime and were allowed almost unlimited freedom—except permission to go beyond the colony's geographic boundaries.

Sara watched them stop a short distance away. Boys and girls played together. She noticed they were dressed like their parents. Even at the end of the day they appeared full of energy. She listened to their endless chatter and laughter.

Even among them, however, she detected a pecking order. Susannah's thirteen-year-old brother, Samuel, appeared to be the leader, although two other boys tried to help. The girls seemed silent listeners and followers. Their role was to reinforce the boys' antics with frequent giggles.

Now they were forming a circle around Joshua, who had appeared leading a brown pony hitched to a homemade cart. Everyone begged for a ride. Holding up his right hand, Joshua softly reminded them no one would get a ride until they all quieted down and formed a line, youngest in front. The children instantly obeyed.

For a half hour Joshua led the pony around the square while the younger children rode in the cart. On each round he was accompanied by an older boy, whom he was teaching the skill of leading the pony safely and gently.

After all the younger children had ridden, they disappeared into their own houses. Joshua worked another half hour with the older boys, walking alongside the cart as he trained each to drive the pony.

The three women watched from their porch step as did some others from their steps. Gradually the women and girls disappeared into their houses to put younger children to bed.

Sara and Susannah went to their room to get ready for bed. Sara lifted her long hair from the collar, which had hidden it all day, and removed the rubber band securing it. She began brushing. Susannah watched.

"I brushed last night and rebraided, so I won't take down my hair again until Saturday when I wash it," she explained, as if reading Sara's unasked question.

"It takes too much time to take down each night and braid again in the morning. Anyway, it doesn't get dirty fast, since it is covered all day."

"How often do you wash your hair?" Sara asked Susannah.

"Every Saturday afternoon. In the morning we get the schoolhouse ready for Sunday church. We have the whole afternoon to ourselves to get ready for Sunday."

This is Thursday night, Sara thought. *I left Toronto on Tuesday and got here on Wednesday. I've been here less than twenty-four hours!*

"What will we do tomorrow?" Sara wondered.

"After breakfast we help Mama clean the house. All

women clean on Friday before they go to work. Then when she goes to the kitchen we will help Anna again in the kindergarten."

Sara remembered one segment of the social group not yet accounted for. "Who takes care of the babies?"

"Their mothers stay home with them. Sometimes if the mother is needed someplace else, one of us older girls will watch the baby."

Sara wondered if they got paid. But why would they need money? She couldn't imagine a world in which some money wasn't necessary. To ask, however, might seem nosy. She'd wait and see. Perhaps she could find out by watching and listening.

She heard Rebekah and Joshua coming up the stairs. They were speaking in German, but their tones sounded worried. Sara looked across at Susannah, puzzled.

Somewhat embarrassed, Susannah explained, "Mama was asking Papa again about the comments against him for buying the pony."

"You mean he was criticized for doing it?" Sara was surprised.

"Some of the members thought it was unnecessary, something we didn't need." Susannah stopped, not sure what more to say.

"How did your father answer?" Sara asked.

"He explained to Mama that he told them that until recently we did all farming with horses. He does not want our boys to grow up and know nothing about horses. They are part of our heritage, too."

"What did your mother say to that?"

"She agrees with Papa. But she is afraid that this disagreement could cause some members to become dissatisfied with Papa's management of the colony."

Susannah paused and chuckled before adding, "She told him that if anyone complains again he should say the pony and cart will be useful when they clean out the hog barns. They can get in where the big tractor can't."

"It might save the colony from having to buy a smaller tractor," Sara added. Both girls giggled.

Suddenly Rebekah appeared in the doorway in her nightgown. "Papa would like to get some rest. You girls will wake up the children with your noise." She spoke firmly but not harshly.

"We're sorry, Mama. We'll turn out the light right now." With that Susannah pulled the chain, plunging the room into darkness.

7

Friday morning after breakfast Susannah and Sara helped Rebekah clean house. Sara couldn't see that any cleaning was necessary.

But Susannah explained that Hutterite women *always* cleaned house on Friday morning. "Cleaning must be done regularly so that houses do not get dirty."

Sara scrubbed and waxed the floor in the washroom, then scoured the lavatory according to Rebekah's instructions. Susannah swept floors and dusted furniture. Rebekah polished windows, then inspected the girls' work. After checking every corner, she excused them to return to the kindergarten while she went to the community kitchen.

Saturday morning Sara and Susannah cleaned the schoolhouse in preparation for two Sunday worship services.

"Our work in here is easy during the summer," Susannah explained as they dusted and straightened the homemade pews.

"Why is that?" asked Sara.

"When school is on, we have to move the work tables and carry the benches stacked there by the wall."

She added, "We have to turn the school pictures to the wall, too."

Sara studied the walls where several maps hung, their backs facing the room. She looked at Susannah questioningly.

"Worldly pictures profane worship," Susannah explained.

Sara tried to imagine what this meant. How could maps profane worship?

"It's our tradition. Our elders have determined it, so we do it."

Sara thought she detected a defensive tone and wondered about it. She hadn't commented, yet she had made her cousin feel uncomfortable.

"Of course," she replied, nodding her head to indicate understanding.

After the noon meal everyone stopped working to prepare for Sunday, both physically and spiritually. The girls got ready to take showers and wash their hair. It took Susannah longer than Sara because she had to unbraid her hair.

Sara passed the time by writing in her journal. When Susannah finished unbraiding her hair, she announced urgently. "We must go to the showers *now*. We have to be out in half an hour so the mothers can use them."

They picked up their towels and a change of clothes and started for the community showers. They entered at one side of the building while boys were entering at the other end. Inside, the showers looked like those in a high school gymnasium, except that there were no lockers. Only open shelves were provided for personal articles.

Sara took a small bottle of shampoo from her pocket and undressed.

"You won't need that," Susannah said. "There are dispensers in each shower stall."

Sara's skin came to life under the intense gush of warm water. The fragrant shampoo worked easily into her hair and rinsed out again, leaving it soft and silky. She could hear the squeals of pleasure and laughter of other girls in other showers. Apparently the Saturday showers were a welcome change after a week of work and daily sponge baths.

The girls dried hurriedly, dressed, and combed their wet hair. Picking up their things, they started back to their own houses. There they met the women on their way to the showers.

When they were back in their room working on their hair, Sara asked, "Is this the way all colonies clean, or just in this one?"

"All colonies do it this way."

"Interesting," Sara mused. Thinking of personal comfort as well as of efficiency, she continued. "I'd think it would be more convenient to have a shower in the washroom of each house. Then you could shower when you wanted."

Susannah shrugged. "What we do is also a part of

our tradition. Getting ready for Sunday the right way is important. We must all do it the same way."

Sara thought about this. She could understand that the weekly showers were a treat, an approved excuse for pampering the body after a week of hard work. Being done by all members on the same day made them a kind of ceremony. Not having showers in each home might also discourage wasting time on personal vanity. *But I'm not so sure I want to live like that!* Sara thought.

Food for Saturday evening supper had been prepared in the morning and was served cold to free the women from spending time in the kitchen during the afternoon. To simplify the clean-up, only a few dishes were used.

The evening was warm and pleasant for outdoor activities. But every family stayed inside their own house. Privately and quietly they prepared their spirits for Sunday.

It was a quiet night in the colony.

8

Sunday morning the breakfast bell rang at seven instead of six forty-five. The girls were already dressed in their Sunday clothes. Susannah's "Bible clothes" were the same style as her weekday clothes, except she didn't wear the large cover-all apron. Her skirt was cut from a plain, dark-blue blend of linen and silk. Her blouse was white, silky crepe.

Sara wore a long, full-gathered dark-blue skirt, flecked with tiny white flowers, and a white blouse. She rolled her braided hair into a bun. She tried to cover it under a sheer, dark-blue kerchief.

Susannah noticed she was having difficulty keeping the bun intact. "Would you like some of my hairpins?"

Sara accepted them happily and pushed them into her hair to keep the bun in place. Satisfied, she wound the kerchief around her head. She tied it above her forehead and turned the ends under. It looked like a turban.

She checked her appearance in her hand mirror. Without makeup she didn't feel fully dressed. But Hutterite women never wore it, so she felt her wearing it might bother them. So far no one had commented on her clothes, so different from theirs. She hoped that meant they were accepting her as she was. She wouldn't feel comfortable dressing like Susannah and Elizabeth. But she'd go without makeup to preserve harmony.

After breakfast the girls returned to their room and waited.

"When will the bell ring calling us to worship?" Sara asked.

"There will not be a bell," Susannah answered. "Sunday *is* for worship. We do not need a bell to tell us so."

Sara realized that again she had spoken out of turn. She remained quiet, waiting for Susannah to make the next move.

As soon as her parents came out of their room, Susannah motioned Sara to follow her. Walking quietly out of the house and across the square, they joined others along the way. People nodded and smiled at each other, but no one spoke as they walked solemnly toward the schoolhouse/church, where others already waited.

There were no babies or young children among the group. Susannah had explained earlier that during worship, school-age children and infants were elsewhere.

Quietly the adults and young people gathered, until everyone was accounted for. Then Susannah and Sara's grandmother, the oldest woman, entered the building. The other women followed, according to age. They sat on the right side of the aisle, the oldest women taking the back bench, the younger women and girls sitting in front. Sara followed Susannah and Elizabeth to the front bench.

Then the men entered according to age and sat on the benches to the left of the aisle. In front of the group was a small, portable platform on which the preacher stood. Between him and the audience was a plain homemade table which served as lectern. To his right sat the assistant preacher and five men, including Joshua. They were the colony's governing council.

Hymns and prayers were followed by two sermons. Sara was surprised to recognize this German. She could understand enough to know that the first sermon was a warning about spiritual living. The second appeared to be about Hutterite history and didn't seem to relate to life today.

She found the singing interesting. There were neither hymnals nor an organ. The preacher sang each line, which worshipers then repeated.

What the singing lacked in quality it made up for in volume. Sara found it rather slow and the tones harsh and piercing.

She was surprised, however, to recognize in the rhythm similarities with the music her father had composed. But he and his group sang much faster, and were always accompanied by several instruments.

The entire service lasted almost two hours, because

today there was also a baptism. Two young men came forward. The preacher questioned them thoroughly. Then the preacher recited additional prayers before laying his hand on the head of each man and sprinkling water on each forehead.

"Have you been baptized?" Sara asked Susannah when they were back in their room after the noon meal.

"Oh, no! We have to be at least seventeen. Most are not baptized until around nineteen or twenty."

"Why?"

"Baptism means we have made a commitment for life, to live our lives as Hutterites."

Sara thought about her father. "You mean that until then you can leave if you want?"

Susannah nodded.

"Do many?"

"Some, but mostly they come back."

"What happens if they decide to leave *after* they've been baptized?"

Susannah shook her head, her face turning sad. "It means they have rejected our ways *after* promising to uphold them. They would not be welcome unless they repented and asked forgiveness."

Sara wondered what her father's situation had been. Had he left before baptism? She hoped so. She knew if she decided to stay, she would eventually have to be baptized. Then there could be no changing her mind.

"Will the young men who were baptized this morning now let their beards grow?"

Susannah shook her head. "No, not until they marry. But now that they are baptized they can marry, if the elders consent."

Both girls were quiet for some time. Then Susannah said, "The service this afternoon will be long, too, because it will include Aunt Mary's engagement ceremony."

Sara tried to hide her surprise. "But I thought you told me last week that her wedding was already planned for next month."

"Yes, we here know and the people in his colony know. But Aunt Mary and her husband-to-be must answer many questions before a group of elders representing both colonies. Then the elders will give their blessing and we can all begin preparing for the wedding."

Sara's continued silence caused Susannah to add, "That, too, is our tradition."

"Of course," Sara nodded. She was still thinking about the unusual worship service. "Why do you sing without an organ and without hymnals?"

"We do not believe we should use musical instruments," Susannah stated firmly.

"But why not?"

Sara needed to know why musical instruments were banned. Perhaps then she could understand the "irreconcilable differences" which had separated her father from his people.

"We believe musical instruments make the human voice appear to be more than God intended. It encourages man to become proud of his abilities."

Susannah paused as if thinking what more to say. "We must obey our elders. They have said that musical instruments give man selfish pleasure and make him forget his Creator."

Sara remembered her father, always playing his guitar, trying out new words and tunes, practicing old ones. In her mind she reviewed songs he had taught her. Perhaps the part of him she missed most was his constant enthusiasm for music.

She suddenly realized that except for the women singing at their work and the singing at worship, she hadn't heard any music since coming. Suddenly she missed her Walkman and radio.

"Don't you miss hearing a radio?" she asked.

Susannah didn't immediately speak. Finally she said, "If you never have something, you don't miss not having it."

She continued, "The young men sometimes bring back transistor radios after they have been in town. When they are found out, the radios are taken from them. I think they miss not having them."

Sara wondered if her father's first guitar had been taken from him. If it was, it must have hurt as much as if they had amputated one of his arms. She didn't want to think about it anymore.

"What about not using songbooks in worship? Is that tradition, too?"

Susannah nodded. "In some places that is changing," she added hopefully.

Then she smiled. "Would you like to hear a story Mama told me about that?"

"Sure." After a morning of total seriousness, Sara yearned for some lightheartedness.

Susannah began. "When Mama was a little girl, one

Sunday a different preacher visited their worship service. While he was leading the singing, his glasses got steamed up. He couldn't see the words in his book.

"So he took off his glasses to wipe them, and said, 'Brothers and sisters, please excuse me, my glasses are fogged up.'

"Then the congregation sang, 'Brothers and sisters, please excuse me, my glasses are fogged up.'

"When they realized what they had done, no one knew what to do next.

"It sounds even funnier in German," Susannah added as her eyes filled with tears of laughter.

Sara imagined the shock those poor people must have experienced. Seeing Susannah laugh so heartily made her feel good, and she joined in the laughter.

The more they laughed, the more their imaginations worked, stirring ever louder laughter.

Suddenly Rebekah appeared in the doorway and stared reprovingly at Susannah. She spoke one word only. But it was clearly a reprimand. "*Gelassenheit.*"

"Sorry, Mama. We forgot," Susannah replied meekly.

Rebekah disappeared. Smarting from the rebuke, Susannah was quiet. Sara didn't understand what Rebekah had said, but she knew they had been scolded. She, too, remained silent to keep herself and Susannah out of further trouble. Finally Susannah spoke in a whisper.

"*Gelassenheit* means keeping our spirits calm and obedient. It is our belief that we must try always to be so, to be ready to accept whatever life gives us.

"It also means to be always at peace with our

neighbor. We must remember it every day, but especially on Sunday.

"By laughing loudly as we did, we showed that our spirits were not right, not ready to receive whatever God might want to tell us."

"I do understand," Sara whispered. This time she felt she really did. *Keep cool*, she thought. Go with the flow. Wasn't that what Susannah meant?

After the engagement service, all school-age children and unbaptized young people had to attend yet another meeting, the German class. The preacher taught them High German, like that used in the worship service. They were required to learn to understand, read, and speak it. Sara already knew some, so she easily understood and followed instructions.

Later she asked Susannah why she couldn't understand the everyday German they spoke to each other.

"That is different German. It is the dialect of our ancestors," Susannah explained.

"They learned it centuries ago when they lived in the Tyrol."

Sara was puzzled. "Where is the Tyrol?"

"I think it is in South Germany. Between Switzerland and Austria," Susannah replied.

Susannah's understanding of geography impressed Sara. Susannah had never traveled further than forty miles from this colony to another one. But on several occasions she had shown clearer knowledge of various countries and regions in the world than Sara had. Yet Sara had traveled all over North America.

9

Sara sat on her bed, leaning against the wall, her pillow propped up behind her. On her raised knees was her open journal. Her private quiet time was nearly half over, but today she hadn't recorded a single word. She looked at Susannah, who sat on her own bed in a similar position, crocheting intently.

Sara envied her cousin's apparent serenity and singleness of purpose. She seemed perfectly content with her life. She had not a worry.

Sara puzzled over her own lack of contentment. This was her twelfth day at Gnadenhof. Everyone had treated her kindly. They had taken her in as one of their own, fed her, provided her with all basic comforts. No one had tried to change her, to convert her to their ideas.

She wondered how much of the goodwill and serenity of others she was responsible for. She had tried to blend into the community willingly, involving herself in all the activities required of others her age. And she had made small concessions in dress. She admitted, however, that she behaved more to satisfy herself than to please others.

She found her new life an adventure. Although naturally cautious, she never avoided new experiences. As for the concessions she had made, she didn't think she was being untrue to herself. Besides, she preferred harmony to conflict wherever she found herself.

She thought about her previous six months in the group home—of the conflicts she had witnessed between other teens, and between teens and the group parents. There had been constant differences of opinion as minds and wills clashed. Teens came and went, but she remained in the first home to which she had been assigned. If Joshua hadn't invited her here, she'd still be there.

The tranquillity here was certainly more agreeable. So why wasn't she completely happy? Was she homesick? But homesick for what? Certainly not the home. It must be for her father and the life they had together. *But that can never again be,* she told herself firmly. *That's WHY I'm here.*

She recalled her counselor's words. "They want you to come for a visit. If you like it there, you can stay." They did like her. She could stay. They were family. Why wasn't that enough?

Susannah interrupted. "It's time we got back to the kitchen." She put away her crocheting.

Sara recalled Jon's advice. Go with the flow. *Gelas-*

senheit. Perhaps she had forgotten. She smiled. In her journal she wrote, "I'm all right *now.* Nothing else matters."

Then images of Jon stirred within her. For an instant she stood with him on the hill overlooking sparkling Lake Superior, listening to his voice. Then she closed the journal and put it on the shelf behind her bed. She felt better already.

Two days later, while she was helping Susannah and Elizabeth set tables, she decided Elizabeth resented her. She had suspected it for some time, ever since Elizabeth had begun speaking to Susannah again in their peculiar German dialect.

She knew that before her arrival the two girls conversed in German. Now, as a courtesy to her, they spoke in English when she was present—which was most of the time. But just now, again, Susannah had answered her cousin in German.

Sara was sure Susannah wasn't aware of what was happening. She wanted to believe Elizabeth wasn't aware of it either, but Sara's intuitions were too strong. She'd have to do something about it.

Sara understood why the problem had developed. Until her arrival the other two girls had been bosom companions, sharing all thoughts and confidences. Sara was an intruder. Now she and Susannah spent their quiet time together. Elizabeth naturally felt left out.

Sara might be partly responsible too. She remembered that at first she did try to bring Elizabeth into conversations through questions and comments. But Elizabeth was shy and needed time to respond. Susannah, on the other hand, became quick to answer for both of them. Maybe she shouldn't have let trouble brew this long.

If she could get Elizabeth alone. . . . That afternoon during quiet time Sara asked Susannah, "Could Elizabeth spend quiet time with us?"

"No," Susannah answered simply. Then she looked across at Sara. "Why do you ask?"

"I don't think Elizabeth likes me," Sara replied.

"What makes you think so?"

"Haven't you noticed? She hasn't spoken to me for several days. And she always speaks to you in German. I think she feels I've come between the two of you."

Susannah didn't answer. She seemed not to know what to say or do.

"Maybe she thinks we're having secrets during our quiet time and feels left out," Sara continued.

"But it isn't true!" Susannah protested.

"We know it isn't, but she doesn't. That's why I thought if she could be with us, like now, she would know."

Susannah shook her head. "Our mamas would not allow it. You and I stay together because we share the same room. But Elizabeth lives in a different house."

"Maybe if I could make her feel she's as important to me as you are—and you could make her feel she's as important to you as I am . . . " Sara thought aloud.

"How can we do that?" Susannah asked.

Sara chose her next words carefully to avoid offending Susannah. "Maybe you could give Elizabeth time to answer some of my questions when the three of us are together. That might make her feel that I think she's important too."

"But Elizabeth doesn't like to talk."

"We have to give her a chance," Sara insisted.

Susannah was silent for a moment, then suggested, "Maybe when we work together, I could be off by myself a bit. Then you could ask her a question and she would have to answer you."

"How could you do that?"

"This week, when we set tables, I could go to the kitchen for more dishes, or go to another table.

"Or tomorrow morning when we pick beans, I could talk to someone else—or pick in a different row," Susannah added excitedly, warming to the idea.

"Would you be willing to do that?"

Susannah nodded.

Sara breathed a sigh of relief. She was sure such an arrangement was worth trying. Perhaps that would also give her a chance to praise Elizabeth for things she did well.

10

Next morning the women washed the breakfast dishes and reset the tables for lunch. Then any women not confined to more pressing work went out to pick beans in the huge field. Susannah remembered her promise. She had taken every opportunity to work apart from Sara and Elizabeth.

To make sure Elizabeth would have to talk to Sara, she asked to be assigned to a different row. At the supervisor's questioning, she explained that she wanted Sara and Elizabeth to get better acquainted. "When I'm around, I talk too much," she explained in German. The supervisor understood and nodded approval.

They had been picking for an hour and Sara's back was beginning to ache. She stood up to rest and watched the ten or more other women bending near the ground, diligently picking beans.

Scanning the field, she counted at least six bushel baskets overflowing with green beans. Stacks of empty baskets stood at strategic spots on the field.

She tried to count the rows of beans left to be picked, but lost track as the rows at the far side of the field blended into each other.

"What are we going to do with all these beans?" she asked.

As usual, Elizabeth waited before answering. "Can them," she said, finally.

"*All* of them?" Sara was surprised. She knew the colony would need lots of food but couldn't imagine having to eat only green beans all winter.

"We sell some to get money for things we buy," Elizabeth explained.

"Where do you sell them?"

"At the Farmer's Market in Winnipeg."

"Will we go sell them?"

"No, the men do that."

Sara noticed that Elizabeth was answering more and more quickly each time. She hoped this meant Elizabeth was becoming more comfortable with her.

"How long will it take us to pick all the beans?"

"Till noon today. After quiet time we will sit under the trees and string them."

Sara thought about Elizabeth's last words. She had offered a second bit of information not asked for. She smiled, encouraged.

"You pick faster than I do—and don't seem to get tired. How do you do it?"

"You get used to it," Elizabeth answered proudly.

"Will we pick again tomorrow?"

"If it doesn't rain. We never pick wet beans, because it makes them get rust spots."

"Oh, I'd never have guessed that!" Sara replied.

After so much talking, Elizabeth seemed to want to stay quiet. Sara also was silent. She hoped Elizabeth might continue the conversation without help.

A quarter of an hour passed. Neither girl said anything. Finally Sara said, "Where do you do all the canning?"

"In the canning room, beside the kitchen. We have two big electric pressure cookers. I will show you."

"When?" Sara wanted very much to keep Elizabeth's attention.

After a long pause, Elizabeth answered. "If you and Susannah come back from your quiet hour before the other women, I—we—can show you."

Noon finally arrived. The women returned to the dining hall.

"Was it all right?" Susannah whispered to Sara while they stood in their places, waiting for the men to enter.

"Yes," Sara nodded.

After the men had all entered, everyone sat down and bowed heads. It was time for opening grace. Then it was time for eating, not talking.

An hour later, during quiet time, Sara told Susannah everything that had happened between her and Elizabeth that morning.

"That was really clever of you to suggest how we could solve the problem," Sara concluded.

Susannah's eyes shone. She certainly didn't want friction between her two cousins. She would have to remember not to talk so much, and give her cousins other chances to work and talk together.

When it was time to meet Elizabeth outside the kitchen, Susannah said, "You go now. I would like to finish this row of crocheting." She didn't look up, but continued her work.

Did Susannah really want to finish the crocheting? Or was she giving the other two girls a chance to be by themselves? Sara wasn't sure.

Elizabeth was standing on the step in front of the kitchen entrance when Sara arrived. "Susannah didn't want to come?" she asked, puzzled.

"She wanted to finish a row of crocheting. She said you could show me. She'll come when the others return."

Elizabeth nodded. She led Sara into a large room filled with canning equipment.

"After we string the beans, we wash them in here." She pointed to two deep sinks.

"This one is for washing them in cold water. That one is for blanching them in hot water."

"What's blanching?" Sara asked.

"Scalding vegetables before freezing or canning them. Blanching takes out crispness so vegetables pack better. It kills bacteria, too, so the vegetables keep."

"Very interesting! Do you can or freeze beans?"

"We can some, we freeze some. For canning, we pack the blanched beans in those jars." She pointed to a table which had dozens of freshly washed jars, turned upside down, draining on huge trays.

"Then we put the jars in these pressure cookers,

and cook them." Elizabeth pointed to two huge vats.

"After the beans are cooked, we seal the jars and cool them. Then we put them away until we need them."

"Where do you keep them?"

"Come, I will show you." She led Sara into a dark, air-conditioned room and switched on the lights.

Sara viewed walls lined with shelves. On the shelves sat dozens and dozens of two-quart jars. Many were empty, but some were filled with fruits and vegetables.

"At the beginning of the season, we still have lots of empty jars," Elizabeth explained.

"These are left from last year." She pointed to a shelf with late summer and early autumn fruits. "We will eat them before the new fruit comes.

"Over here we have the new things." She pointed to a shelf with jars of canned peas.

"The beans will go here." She pointed.

"What do you freeze?" Sara asked.

"Some of everything. If it can be frozen. Lots of peas, because they keep better frozen. All berries."

"Where are your freezers?"

"Here." Elizabeth led into an inner sanctum where large freezers completely hid two walls.

The state-of-the-art equipment overwhelmed Sara. How did they afford it all?

"Do you actually save money by growing and preserving all your food?" she asked Elizabeth.

Elizabeth thought awhile.

"Our ancestors always grew their own food. We have land and lots of people to work the land, to grow and prepare the food.

"This keeps us from having to leave the colony to make a living, and mixing with people who are not Hutterites.

"It makes us work together. It is our tradition to live and work in community, apart from the world."

Sara was surprised at Elizabeth's ability and willingness to talk of Hutterite beliefs and practices. In spite of Susannah's insistence that she didn't, Elizabeth liked to talk when given a chance, Sara realized.

"Don't you ever leave the colony?" she asked.

"Our men do, sometimes. They have to do some business with the world, like sell the goods we don't need—and buy things we need and cannot raise or make ourselves."

How do they hold it all together? Sara wondered. They certainly didn't live in the primitive ways their ancestors must have had. Their up-to-date equipment proved that.

Yet they shared all things in common, lived in community, kept their lives separate from people who weren't Hutterites. They had no television and radio sets, musical instruments, record players, phones. So old-fashioned and so modern, all wrapped together.

How long can they make it all keep working? Sara wondered.

She thought again of her father. How much conflict did he cause with his music?

"Some young people leave, but most return," Susannah had told her. Her father hadn't. Now where did she fit?

11

Sara lay wide-awake in her bed that night after lights out. She wondered what the women had been talking about all afternoon while working with the beans. She wished she could understand their German. Whatever the subject was, the talk was more animated than usual—talk filled with concern.

She heard Susannah turning in her bed and decided she wasn't asleep either. Leaning over, she whispered, "Psst!"

"Yah?" Susannah whispered back.

"What were the women talking about this afternoon?"

"The coming Division," Susannah answered.

"The what?"

"The Division of the colony."

Sara silently tried to puzzle out what Susannah meant. Finally she gave up and asked, "What kind of a division?"

Susannah thought a moment before whispering back. "Our group is growing too big. We are one hundred and thirty-three now. Our tradition requires that we not grow to more than one hundred and fifty. So before then we must divide."

"Why can't you grow larger?"

"If the colony is too big, people don't get to know each other like a family. Our elders say it is too hard to manage and keep everyone equally busy."

"But you don't have to divide right away, do you?"

"No, but we grow fast. Aunt Mary will leave next month when she marries. But later this fall two of our young men will marry and bring their wives here. Also, you probably noticed that we will have two more babies before the end of the year."

Sara had heard and noticed that Hutterite families tended to be larger than the national average. She assumed that the couples marrying this year would carry on the tradition and start their own families immediately.

"We must buy more land before we can divide," Susannah continued. "Then we have to divide everything to share with the new colony. This takes time. The managers have started looking for land."

No wonder the women were concerned, Sara thought. The close-knit group would be broken up. They had depended on each other for all their emotional and social support. A change or transfer would be as hard on them as on a family where a parent was transferred to another city, and the other parent and children had to make all new friends.

"Will you have to go?"

"No one knows yet who will go and who will stay," Susannah answered.

"When will you know?"

"After the land is bought and the equipment divided."

"Then what?" Sara persisted.

"The families will be divided into two groups, according to age and ability to work, so all work in each colony can be done."

"Who decides who belongs in each group?"

"Our elders, by drawing lots. Those in one group stay with the preacher. The other group goes with the assistant preacher."

Sara thought about how it might feel to have her fate decided by someone drawing a number out of a hat, or by the turn of a card. Life seemed like a gamble enough without deliberately submitting to a lottery.

"How do they decide which group will stay and which will go?"

"By lot, too." This time Susannah didn't whisper.

Immediately there was a knock on the wall between their and the parents' rooms, demanding silence.

Susannah whispered, "I'll tell you more tomorrow during quiet hour if you still have questions." Then she turned her face to the wall and closed her eyes. But Sara remained awake a long time.

The next morning, after breakfast and dishes, the women returned to picking beans. Elizabeth was quiet. Sara assumed she was thinking about the Division and wondering whether she and Susannah would be separated.

Finally she asked, "Are you worried that the Division will separate you and Susannah?"

Elizabeth shrugged and paused. "We must not get too attached to any person or place," she said firmly.

After a long pause she added, "We would be allowed to visit each other, sometimes." She sighed.

Sara noticed that all the women were quiet today. Her heart went out to them. They, too, had to give up things, end relationships, suffer separations. Their lives were really not very different from hers.

At midmorning the children descended on the group, chattering like a flock of saucy birds. They spoke excitedly in German, each trying to talk above the others.

One of the women hushed them and asked questions, allowing only one child at a time to speak. Sara and Elizabeth were near enough to hear what they were saying, but only Elizabeth could understand.

After the children were ordered to go elsewhere to play, Elizabeth said to Sara, "Jake is sick."

Sara wondered who Jake was. She hadn't met any of the males, except for Joshua and Grandfather. Elizabeth, realizing she was puzzled, explained, "The pony."

Sara thought about the little brown horse that pulled the cart most evenings, giving the children rides and allowing the older boys to drive him. He was a great favorite among all the children. His health and welfare were undoubtedly as important to them as their own family members' health.

"What seems to be the matter?" Sara asked.

Elizabeth shrugged. "He won't eat and slobbers.

The children are to stay away from him."

Sara knew the adults were thinking of rabies. But would rabies be a problem in Manitoba? Unlike southern Ontario, Manitoba wasn't almost surrounded by water. Probably wild animals could come out of the northern lake country, too, but they wouldn't be trapped in a small area, free to infect domestic animals, and then the humans tending and petting them.

She knew rabies always led to painful death. She remembered an instance on a farm outside of Toronto where a friend's pony had gotten rabies. No one knew when or how, but by the time it was diagnosed, at least fourteen people had petted and tended the pony. They all had to be vaccinated; some had suffered painful side effects.

She could hear worry-talk in small groups around the field. When the talk was near enough for Elizabeth to hear, she would tell Sara what had been said. Doc Epp, the vet, had been called. If the pony had rabies, it would have to be destroyed. All who had touched him would need vaccinations. That would include all the children.

"How soon will they know?" Sara asked.

Elizabeth shrugged. They'd have to await Doc Epp's diagnosis.

During the quiet hour, Sara stared at her open journal. Her thoughts seemed tied in knots. Her mind couldn't unravel and transfer them to paper. Susannah, sitting on the opposite bed, crocheted quietly, sighing from time to time.

Concerns about the impending Division seemed to have fled. But nothing more could be said or done

about the pony until Doc Epp had given his opinion,—
and he wasn't due until evening.

During the afternoon the three girls sat in the
shade with some of the women and snapped beans.
Meanwhile other women canned them in the kitchen.
Everyone worked in silence, waiting for evening and
Doc Epp. Each woman tried to calm her own spirit.

After the evening meal and chores, the women sat
on their porches and waited. The children, their simple world shattered, sat quietly with their mothers
and older sisters. The men accompanied Doc Epp to
the barn to see the pony. Later they returned and
stood talking by his station wagon.

At dusk, the women took the children indoors
while the men talked outside. Finally Joshua entered
his house and spoke with Rebekah. While the girls
got ready for bed, Susannah told Sara the news.

Doc Epp was puzzled. The symptoms weren't quite
right for rabies, but he couldn't be sure. So Jake
would have to be isolated from the other animals and
the children until Doc Epp could figure it out.

"How will Doc Epp know if the pony has rabies?"
Sara asked.

"If he does, Jake will die. Then his brain will be
sent to a laboratory in Winnipeg."

"How long before he dies?" Sara asked.

"Five days or a week."

Sara had heard that death by rabies was extremely
painful. The victim couldn't drink water but fever
caused constant thirst.

"Wouldn't it be better to put him out of his misery
before then?"

"They have to be sure he has rabies because the vaccination can be hard for some people." Susannah quietly added, "If all the children have to be vaccinated, it could be very bad for us." Sighing, she turned her face to the wall.

Sara stared at the ceiling. There the lights from the square, screened by leaves, cast menacing shadows—like those on moving waters whose depths have not been tested.

12

Work for the next two days proceeded as usual. Friday morning the women cleaned house. Saturday morning the girls prepared the schoolhouse for Sunday worship. During the afternoon they prepared for Sunday.

After shampoos and showers, Sara asked Susannah if she could see the rest of the compound. Although she had now been in the colony more than two weeks, she had seen only the area in which the women worked. She knew much activity took place in other buildings and areas.

Susannah suggested that they ask Elizabeth's older brother Eli to show them around. Sara was pleased; she hadn't met any of the young men. She realized that living and moving about in a world of only women left something to be desired.

Eli was pleased to meet his visiting cousin and

show off his masculine expertise. He would be happy to guide them through the men's areas.

First he took Sara and Susannah to the farm implement garage and machine shop. Then to the implement storage yard and the electrical shop. Sara knew little about such things, but Eli proudly explained all. The abundance of modern equipment impressed Sara. Definitely state-of-the-art! No horse-drawn machinery here.

On the way to the barns Eli detoured slightly so Sara could see the cemetery. She looked about at the dozen or more small, upright markers. They were beautifully made of stained oak with hand-carved lettering, covered with clear wood preservative. The earliest date of death was 1918.

"This is our great-great-grandfather's grave." Eli pointed to the first grave in the upper right-hand corner. "He died the same year our people took refuge after fleeing from South Dakota."

"What were they fleeing?" Sara asked.

Eli thought before answering. "After the United States entered the First World War, the government began calling Hutterite men for military service."

He paused. "We are conscientious objectors. When our men refused to undertake military duties, they were treated badly."

"What was done to them?"

"All sorts of things. They were chased across fields by soldiers on motorcycles. Some were thrown into cold water, or beaten. Some died." Eli didn't seem to want to say more.

"So they moved into Canada," Sara concluded.

Eli nodded. "They did not want to cause any trouble. They just wanted to be left alone to run their farms and raise their families."

All were silent with their own thoughts. Sara pondered freedom. Freedom to worship according to conscience. That was all these people wanted.

Yet how was this freedom to be maintained? Surely the soldiers would rather have stayed home too, attending to business and families.

"Our great-great-grandmother died three years later. This is her grave." Eli pointed to the third grave in the first row.

Sara wondered about the grave between them. "They didn't bury couples together?"

Eli shook his head. "We still bury people in the order of their deaths."

Sara looked at Susannah in surprise.

"We are all *one* family," Susannah explained.

"Come! We will go see the animals," Eli announced abruptly. He led them to pig barns. There were three: the dry sow barn, the farrowing barn, and the feeder hog barn. The countless pigs, ranging from tiny, lively pink piglets to huge slow-moving sow mothers, overwhelmed Sara.

"What do you do with them all?" she asked.

"Sell them. Pigs are our main source of income."

Sara had wondered how the colony paid for all the modern equipment in the farm garage and storage area, electric shop, and hog barns—not to mention the kitchen, laundry, and bathhouse. Now she knew.

"Would you like to see the chickens and the geese?" asked Eli.

"I want to see everything!" Sara answered emphatically.

"We are limited in the numbers of chickens and geese we can raise. The chickens because we do not have a marketing quota—which is permission to market a significant amount of something—for chickens and eggs. And the geese because not everyone likes roast goose."

Sara had been comparing Eli's with the women's use of language. She knew the men left the colony frequently to conduct business in town. It showed in their speech. Eli was more articulate than either Susannah or Elizabeth. And they spoke better English than their mothers.

"This is the brooder house where we raise young chickens. Over there is the hen laying house. We butcher the young roosters for ourselves and the pullets become laying hens."

"Do you sell lots of eggs?" Sara asked.

"What we don't use, yes. We could sell many more, but without a quota we are limited to selling only a small amount."

"Do you have a quota for hogs?"

"None is required," Eli answered. "Over here is the geese area. They like water, so we have them close to the creek.

"Hutterites, geese, and creeks all go together," he added jokingly.

After looking into the goose hatchery, the goose-starting barn and the goose-laying barn, Sara asked, "What do you do with all the geese?"

"Butcher them just before Thanksgiving. Some people prefer roast goose to turkey during the holidays. We eat goose then, too, and for Sunday dinners. We save the feathers and the women clean them and make them into pillows."

"We always have more orders for pillows than we can fill," Susannah added.

"You might get to help in the pillow room this summer," Elizabeth added.

"What do you do there?" Sara asked Elizabeth.

"We wash and dry the feathers. Then we strip them. We make pillow tubes and fill them with feathers."

Sara was pleased at how well Elizabeth was talking to her while with others. She thanked Susannah with her eyes for giving Elizabeth this chance. Susannah smiled.

"You don't have cows?" Sara asked Eli.

"Just enough for our own milk and meat," he answered. "To sell milk, you need a quota, too. We don't have one."

At that moment they met Eli's father and Joshua coming out of the dairy barn. Each was carrying two pails of milk. Eli's father spoke to him in German and Eli answered in German, too.

"He wants me to throw some hay to the cows and check on the horse before Doc Epp comes," he explained for Sara's benefit.

"How is the pony?" Sara asked, glad to have this opportunity to discuss the subject.

"Do you want to come see?"

"Are we allowed?" She was surprised.

"If you don't get in the pen with him, or touch him, there is no danger to you," Eli explained. "Unless you get his saliva on an opening in your skin."

"How does he look?" Sara's heart went out to sick or helpless animals. She wasn't sure she wanted to see the sick pony.

"Frankly, no worse than two days ago. It is a surprise."

They were interrupted by Doc Epp's station wagon, which had just driven into the compound and was creeping toward the barn.

"Hello! How's our patient today?" Doc Epp asked.

"About the same, I guess," Eli answered.

Doc Epp shook his head. "I don't understand. There should have been a change by now. Well, let's go have a look." He strode into the barn, followed by Eli.

The girls went as far as the barn door, watching the vet and Eli stand at the horse's stall.

"This doesn't look like a rabid pony to me!" Doc exclaimed.

"May we come in?" Susannah called to Eli.

Before he could answer, Doc Epp said, "Sure! Come see a miracle."

What the girls saw was a bright-eyed pony with no lather on his mouth. He gave a friendly nicker.

"I've never seen anything like it. I just don't understand it," Doc Epp said.

"It looks like he has been drinking water," Eli said, pointing to the almost empty bucket.

"Whatever he had, it couldn't have been rabies," Doc commented. He jumped over the paneled enclosure and examined the pony carefully.

Then he checked Jake's feed box. "He's been eating, too." He raked his fingers through the remaining grain to check what the horse had been fed.

Suddenly he stopped. "What's this?" He held up a stone, irregular in shape, but larger than a plum.

"Probably something the children dropped in when they were petting him," Eli answered.

"This could have caused the problem," Doc Epp mused. "He might have gotten this stone wedged back in his jaw while he was eating.

"He couldn't dislodge it so he couldn't close his mouth. That caused him to slobber." Doc shook his head.

"I remember something similar happening to a dog once. He got a large, irregular shaped bone wedged in his jaw, and I had to remove it."

"If we had only known, we could have done that for Jake," Eli commented.

"Sure," Doc agreed. "I should have thought of that possibility, but it never occurred to me that might be Jake's problem. Horses don't chew bones. Do they?" He gave Jake a friendly pat. "And . . . there was the possibility he might have become rabid, although his symptoms were not entirely what I would have expected.

"Anyway a rabid animal has to be observed from a distance since treatment is impossible and bodily contact with one is always dangerous."

"Then the pony is all right?" Sara asked.

"Right as rain," Doc assured her. "You might speak to the children about the seriousness of bringing objects into Jake's stall. Small rocks, toys, string or plastic can all be hazardous to animals. Especially when the objects get in their food."

The three girls went immediately to the kitchen to

tell the women. Within ten minutes everyone in the colony had heard. At supper, everyone was smiling.

In their own house Joshua and Rebekah talked about it at length, in German.

While they were getting ready for bed Susannah said, "Papa and Mama are relieved. When the pony was sick, they feared God was punishing Papa for buying the pony without the elders' permission."

"But the pony is fine!"

"That is why they are relieved. If all the children had to be vaccinated, Papa would have been held responsible." Susannah heaved a sigh of relief and switched off the light.

Even in the darkness, Sara knew by Susannah's breathing that she had fallen asleep immediately. But Sara couldn't sleep. She stared instead at the ceiling where the light from outside, screened by the moving leaves, cast its dancing shadows.

13

The second half of July went fast. Sara had settled into the daily routine, which also provided several new activities. After the beans were all picked and processed, the girls and some of the women picked raspberries and cherries. As fast as they brought them to the kitchen, the women washed and froze them.

When they weren't working with fruit or garden produce, the women were preparing for Mary's wedding—scheduled for the morning worship service Sunday, August 6.

Since the members of the groom's colony would be present for the ceremony and the dinner to follow, the women had to prepare twice as much food as usual. They baked, packed, and froze dozens and dozens of cookies and pastries. They made huge casseroles of mixed vegetables.

During quiet times, every woman was sewing presents for the bride. She wouldn't have to furnish a kitchen but would have to bring her own linens. The woman trimmed many sheets, pillowcases, and towels with hand-crocheted lace and embroidery. Now the bride would have a respectable personal dowry, showing that all the sisters held her in high esteem and wanted to give their finest work to her.

There was also to be a surprise gift from all the women, an elaborate quilt. For many months some of the women had been meeting in secret, planning and designing the quilt top. It was to show the general history of the two colonies as well as include some personal history of the bride and groom. The individual blocks had been farmed out to be finished in secret during private time.

The separate blocks had to be sewn together for the top. Then the top, interlining, and lining had to be tacked together and mounted on frames so the quilting could begin. Quilting would require at least half a dozen women working together for three or four long evenings. How could they do all this without Mary's knowledge?

Since the women rarely left the colony, it was difficult to find a believable way to divert Mary from the project. Before each working session one or two women were assigned to watch over and keep her company during quilting hours.

They helped her prepare her accessories, which were quite simple. Sara learned that Hutterite women don't wear the traditional white bridal gown and veil. No honeymoon follows the wedding, so no traveling clothes are needed. But every bride does sew new

Sunday clothes for the ceremony. She also makes a supply of dresses, aprons, and underwear to take her through her first years of marriage. Mary would be well supplied.

Since the quilting frames were set up in Rebekah's parlor, Sara watched the activity from beginning to end. The women encouraged, even pressed her, to take a needle and thread and add her stitches. She fussed that her stitches were uneven and longer than the others. But the women insisted she'd learn. The frequent pricks of her unskilled needle roughened her fingertips, but she didn't complain.

Weather on the day of the ceremony was perfect. The brilliant golden sun shone in the clear azure sky. The air was dry and cool, in contrast to July's hot humid days. After morning worship and the marriage ceremony, the men moved the picnic tables out of the dining room to the nearby shade of the square. Women brought blankets from their houses and spread them for the children.

The men of the host colony carried out the hot food to a central table from which they served it. Other men dipped ice-cold lemonade from huge canning vats into waiting cups. The women helped the children fill their plates and settled them on the blankets. Then the adults filed past the food. Today they mixed and chatted freely with each other.

There was no afternoon worship service as the two colonies mingled to celebrate the marriage which had again confirmed their unity. Late in the afternoon all members of the visiting colony left for home in a bus and several station wagons.

Mary and her new husband, Benjamin, were the last to leave. She gave each of her sisters a hug and thanked them for their gifts. Then she and Benjamin got into the last station wagon, along with her boxes of clothes and gifts, and drove off.

All the adults of Gnadenhof pitched in to clean up. Some men carried the tables back into the dining hall. Others carried food containers and dirty dishes back into the kitchen, where the women washed and set them for the next meal.

Evening arrived in silence as families retired to their own houses, meditating on the activities which had made this a special Sunday.

Susannah went to sleep immediately, exhausted from all the unusual activity. But Sara remained awake, pondering everything that had happened.

She thought about Mary and Benjamin. There had been no exchange of rings, no joining of hands during the ceremony, no public kiss. She knew their courting hadn't been a long process. They had known each other since childhood. They had had to get approval for marriage from their parents and also from the governing bodies of each colony.

They had probably never spent time alone until this afternoon on their drive back to their new home. Tomorrow Mary would join the women in the colony. Benjamin would join the men. They would see each other only after each day's work was over. Then the morning bell would separate them again. Until they had children who had reached age fifteen, who could then eat with them, they would probably eat at different tables.

Sara tried to imagine a life with personal relationships with men so highly structured. Such an arrangement defied her innermost dreams and yearnings. She wondered how they tolerated it, especially the women.

Then she realized they knew no other courtship and marriage styles. She wondered about her own parents. How had they met? This, too, was something that her father hadn't told her before his sudden death.

Her thoughts drifted to Jon. She imagined his eyes brushing hers. She was too young to think of marriage—but did she want someone else deciding for her what part Jon or someone else should play in her love life? She didn't know. Dating in the outside world was fun, but it could be confusing. Hutterite courtship didn't seem like much fun, but it was safe.

Thinking about this made her suddenly aware of her present situation. The summer was more than half over. She would have to make an important decision in the next two or three weeks. She would have to decide her future.

14

Sara noticed the days were turning shorter. The sun was slower to appear in the morning and quicker to disappear at night. Summer was fast running out. Life in the colony was filled with preparations for winter.

She felt a growing anxiety about her own future. As she worked with the women, she spent less and less effort trying to understand what they were discussing. She asked fewer questions about their customs. What she really wanted to know was about her father's relationship with them and the details of his departure.

Since her arrival, the only mention of her father had been that she and he looked alike. Thinking about it angered her. Were they deliberately keeping important information from her? Then she recalled that any information she had asked for had been given.

But her sources had been mainly Susannah and Elizabeth. They would tell her what they knew. But she doubted they would know anything about her father. She would at least ask. But how could she avoid sounding overly inquisitive or rude?

One day in their room during quiet hour Sara wondered, "How long before I came here did you know about me?" She was trying to write in her journal while Susannah was knitting a sweater.

"A few days," Susannah answered without looking up from her knitting.

Sara felt rising anger. Then she remembered she hadn't known about Susannah's existence until six weeks ago, when Rebekah had led her into this room and introduced them.

"What do you know about my father?" she asked boldly.

Susannah continued to knit for some time before answering, "He left the colony when he was young." She paused. "He chose a life of music."

"When did you learn that?" Sara pushed on.

"When I heard you were coming." Both girls were silent.

Finally Susannah said, "Papa could tell you what you want to know." She hesitated. "If it is something you should know."

Susannah was right, of course. Joshua would know, but how to approach him? He had seemed pleasantly civil to her on the night of her arrival but hadn't spoken directly to her since. She didn't know what he'd think or how he'd act if she asked him a question. Even Susannah spoke to him only if he had spoken to her first.

"I will tell Mama what you are asking," Susannah

promised. "She will talk to Papa. They will decide what you should know."

For the next quarter of an hour the girls were silent. Finally Susannah put away her knitting. "We must go back to work," she said.

That afternoon they spent in the shade under the trees. For a time they husked corn ears they had picked in the forenoon. Other women cut the corn off the cobs, in preparation for freezing.

Then they exchanged jobs. Sara spent the next hour standing beside the table, holding an ear of corn in one hand and a sharp knife in the other, cutting juicy golden kernels off the white cobs.

Other women worked in the kitchen packing the corn into large plastic bags. Sara was reminded again of what she had noticed since the first day. No one worked at any one job long. Difficult jobs were shared equally with less difficult ones. Every effort was made to keep work from becoming tedious, to keep muscles from becoming sore.

For several days the women worked with the corn. They picked it in the morning, then husked, cut, packed, and froze it in the afternoon.

Then it was time to pick and can peaches. Almost a week had passed since Susannah had promised to talk with Rebekah about Sara's questions. Sara waited impatiently.

In the meantime, she spent her private time recalling her experiences and analyzing herself in light of them. She admired the tranquil composure of the people and their commitment to each other. She was grateful they had accepted her into their family and hadn't tried to change her. She had come to love and accept Susannah as the sister she never had. She respected the efficient and unique system by which the colony was run.

This summer had been indeed interesting. She had found a family to help her adjust to losing her father. And she had learned much about herself, and her reactions to a vastly different way of life.

She envied the well-planned, cradle-to-grave security the colony provided its members. It could be hers if she chose to accept it. But she knew that she wasn't ready to commit her life to it now—if ever.

She wanted to return to the outside world, to school, to music, to travel . . . maybe to Jon. She didn't know yet what she wanted to do with her life. But there were so many paths she wanted to explore. All would require time, money, and—for some years yet—adult supervision. She was resourceful and adaptable. But she wasn't, at fifteen, ready to face the world by herself.

If she left several weeks from now, what could she expect? Children's Aid would keep her until she was sixteen. That would mean another group home. Then another agency would help until she was eighteen.

But what limitations would they place on her? Would they let her go to college? *They'll probably want me to be practical, go into work needing less school*, she thought. This, too, would limit her explorations.

Her anxiety and indecision stirred anger—anger at the deal life had given her. Why had her father left her when he went on that last tour? Why did that plane have to crash, taking the whole group who had been her family and security?

She lashed out at herself, too. *Why can't I be like Susannah, and be happy here the rest of my life?*

Then she remembered something Susannah had said earlier, "If you never have something, you don't miss not having it." That was her problem. She had had so much of everything. Freedom of choice. Experiences. Love and security. She wanted to keep it all.

But common sense reminded her no one can keep it all. Life requires choices. Each choice *for* something requires a choice *against* something else. Her father, realizing that, had made his choice. She needed to know more about him and what happened when he made that choice. How was she to find out?

Just before quiet hour Rebekah handed her a sealed envelope. "This came in the mail today," she explained.

Sara opened the letter anxiously, wondering who would be writing to her. It was from Jon.

Hi,
How is your summer? Work here on the farm keeps me busy from before sunup to after sunset. I'm really getting a tan. Hope you're happy getting to know your family. Have been looking for a letter from you. Maybe you've been too busy to write?? Let me know what your autumn plans are.
As always,
Jon

Sara was puzzled by the letter's brevity. Jon liked to talk so much. Why hadn't he written more? How was she to interpret the two question marks? Did he really think she was too busy to write? Was he angry because she hadn't written?

Or was he giving her a clue that her mail might be censored before it reached her? Had he decided not to write anything which might create problems for her?

She was embarrassed, and annoyed with herself for not having written. She had thought about writing several times, wanting to tell him what she was doing and thinking. She knew her concern that her mail might be checked was what had stopped her. She was sure Joshua and Rebekah checked Susannah's mail. Maybe they would check hers, too.

Jon's letter had been delivered to her sealed, so her fears had apparently been unjustified. Now she was filled with too much confusion and indecision to write.

She yearned to see Jon again and explain everything. Today she couldn't even write in her journal. She lay on her back and stared at the ceiling.

Susannah sat on the other bed, knitting intently but casting sly glances at Sara from time to time. Finally she spoke. "The letter—bad news?"

"No." Sara continued to stare at the ceiling.

Susannah stared thoughtfully at Sara. *She can probably tell I'm upset,* Sara thought, *but I'm too confused to let her in.*

Finally Susannah said, "I told Mama what you asked. She will mention it to Papa when he isn't so busy."

Sara let the relief and hope on her face tell Susannah she had said the right thing.

Sara thought about Joshua. As the colony's business manager, he had to make so many difficult decisions.

She recalled the rabies scare. He had bought the pony simply to maintain tradition and teach the young men how to work with horses. The pony had brought the children joy and provided a bond between Joshua and the older boys. Yet some members had criticized his decision.

Then when the pony appeared to be sick, the colony blamed him for possibly introducing rabies. Thinking of the responsibilities Joshua faced, Sara felt ashamed of herself.

She had been spending too much time and energy worrying about herself. She hadn't been going with the flow, as Jon had advised. *Gelassenheit* was difficult to achieve. She looked over at Susannah and smiled. "You've all been kind. Thank you."

Susannah smiled as she put down her knitting. Then she stood and opened her arms to Sara. Sara put her arms around Susannah. Then Susannah returned to her knitting, and Sara wrote in her journal.

That evening, after the little brothers were in bed, Rebekah appeared at the door. "Susannah, Papa wants to talk to Sara," she announced.

Then she said to Sara, "Come with me."

The two cousins looked knowingly at each other. Sara followed Rebekah into the parlor. Joshua was waiting.

15

Joshua stood when the two women entered. He motioned Sara toward the settee. Rebekah left the room. Sara's heart beat as wildly as it had that first night when she waited for Rebekah to return with the snack. She hadn't been in this room nor spoken to Joshua since that memorable time.

He smiled. "So. You have been asking about your papa. What would you like to know?"

Sara tried to swallow the lump suddenly filling her throat. How should she begin? Questions rushed from every part of her brain. She tried to condense them into one clear thought which would explain her concern.

"Father never told me much about his life here . . . or his leaving." She paused, hoping Joshua would take over.

He didn't. So she continued, "When I was little and

asked questions, he'd say, 'I'll tell you when you're older and can understand.'

"I learned not to ask. I knew he'd tell me when he thought I was ready . . . but he never got a chance." She swallowed hard.

Joshua nodded and remained silent. He seemed to be thinking what he would say to this niece, the daughter of his beloved brother. Then he began.

"He was my older brother by less than two years. I loved him. When he left, I thought my life would end." Joshua worked to control his voice.

Sara, feeling his pain, tried to help. "When did he become interested in music? Did that cause a lot of trouble before he left?" she asked pointedly.

Her directness left Joshua speechless. Sara sensed his shock but gently persisted. "Please," she begged, "This is important to me. I must know."

Finally Joshua spoke. "It might be easier if I told it like a story. After I finish you can ask questions about anything I haven't explained. Would that be all right?"

Sara nodded. She liked stories. And she welcomed not having to ask a hundred questions.

* * *

Joshua's Story

I must have been about eleven, your father maybe thirteen. It was summer. We had been told to cut the weeds in the boundary fence where the mower didn't reach. We each had a small hand scythe.

Near one part of our boundary there was a house. It isn't there anymore. Old man Brown lived there then. He was a good man but not a very good farmer. While others worked, he played his music. That day the windows were open; we could hear a guitar.

We were still children and without permission to go beyond our own boundaries. But Jonas, your papa, said, "Let's go closer so we can hear better."

I was afraid to disobey Papa, but Jonas was older. I knew if we were caught, he would get the punishment. I would just get scolded. Anyway, by the time I had thought this out, Jonas had already jumped over the fence and was almost at the house. I followed.

We stood there beside the window for a long time, just listening to the music. I forgot we were supposed to stay quiet. I said something to Jonas out loud.

Old Brown heard us. He came to the window and looked out. "Well!" he said. "A couple of little Hutterites. You like music, eh?"

"We were just listening to you play," Jonas explained. "Can we see your guitar?"

"Sure, sure. Come on in," he invited.

It was the first time either of us had ever been in a house that wasn't in the colony. It looked strange. There was junk lying everywhere. Musical instruments, parts of instruments, sheets of music. You see, he didn't have a wife anymore to do the housework.

Jonas did not notice the mess. All he saw were the instruments which had always been forbidden us. He looked at them like a hungry child looks at good-smelling food the women have just prepared but told him not to touch. Especially the guitar.

Old Brown saw and understood his look. "Go on, boy," he said. "Pick it up."

Jonas looked at him as if he didn't believe his ears. Then he picked up the guitar as gently as a new father picks up his firstborn for the first time.

He started fingering the strings. Playing music seemed to just come to him. It wasn't like what Old Brown had played, but it was music.

Old Brown shook his head. "Say, who taught you how to hold a guitar and pluck its strings?"

Jonas looked puzzled, as if he wondered himself. His heart was so full of music he couldn't stop playing. He kept trying out new sounds.

After a few minutes Old Brown said, "Here, let me show you a couple of chords."

He picked up the guitar. "This is C Chord." He strummed for a few minutes, then handed the guitar back to Jonas. "Here, boy. Can you do that?"

Jonas took the guitar. On the first try he played exactly what Old Brown had played. Then he changed it several different ways and tapped his foot to it.

"Okay," Old Brown said. "Give me the guitar. I want to show you something else." Then he played something else which I could tell was much harder.

Jonas took the guitar a second time. Again he did exactly what Old Brown had done.

Old Brown was so surprised he didn't have any words for a while. Then he said, "Boy, you sure are a natural musician."

He shook his head. "What a pity," he mumbled to himself.

Then he changed. "You boys better get back on your own land and do whatever your pa told you to do." He put the guitar up on a high shelf and turned us toward the door.

"Can we come back sometime to hear you play?" Jonas asked.

"Sure. If you aren't afraid your pa will skin you alive." Again he shook his head as if he didn't want to believe what he had just seen and heard.

I knew we had done something forbidden, but I would not tell. We went back to Old Brown's house several times that summer.

When winter came, it was harder to find excuses to leave our grounds. Sometimes Jonas slipped away by himself. I would pretend he was still around here somewhere. Always Old Brown let Jonas play. He fixed a second guitar from parts lying around. Then he and Jonas played duets.

Jonas had been going to Old Brown for more than a year when the second winter came. He knew it would be harder to sneak away to practice. He did not want me to have to tell lies about where he was. So he asked Old Brown one day if he could bring his guitar back and hide it here.

Old Brown told him, "Sure, if you're willing to take the consequences. You know, I don't want no trouble with your people."

For the next two winters Jonas hid the guitar and played it almost every day. He had to change the hiding place often. Whenever new work was assigned, he would consider whether it would be easier but still safe to hide the guitar somewhere else. He also started writing words to songs he made up.

I knew how much his music meant to him. And I was growing more and more afraid someone would find out what he was doing. I offered to take over some of his chores so he would have more time to play. I even tried to think of new hiding places. I was as guilty of going against our teachings as he.

Then it was early spring, after the second winter of hiding the guitar. Jonas and I had been told to check the fences at the farthest end of the field so we could let the cows graze on the volunteer wheat. The fences needed more work than we had expected. We stayed out to fix them.

We got back late so Papa started our chores. When he dug into the hay, he found the guitar. He did not say anything when we returned and joined him. But we knew what had happened. The three of us finished the chores in silence.

As we were going in for supper, Papa said, "After we eat, I want to talk to you boys at our house."

We had been out in the cold air all afternoon. We came back very hungry, but now we both had lost our appetites. After the meal, when we were going to our house, Jonas said, "Don't say anything. Let me talk."

Papa was waiting in the parlor. Mama and the girls were still at the kitchen helping with dishes and setting tables. Our little brother was playing somewhere with the other schoolchildren. Jonas and I stood inside the door, waiting for Papa to speak.

He did not invite us to sit. "I found something in the hay today," Papa began. "It grieves me more than I can say. What can you tell me about it?"

Jonas said, "It's mine."

"And where did you get it?" Papa asked.

"From Old Brown. I asked if I could have it."

"You knew it is against our teaching but still did

it!" Papa's voice was disgusted and disappointed.

"I knew but couldn't help myself."

"It is not enough to confess to me. Next Sunday after worship you must confess to the people what you have done. You must ask their forgiveness. Then in your private prayers you must ask our Creator to take this evil desire from you."

Jonas nodded.

"What do you think I should do with you for your disobedience?" Papa asked.

"Whatever you feel is right, Papa," Jonas answered.

Papa thought before he spoke. "You are too old to spank like I would punish a child," he said. "You have a choice. Repent of your evil thoughts and desires. Commit all your life to our ways. Or lose your place among us."

I knew then we had lost him. It was only a matter of when he would leave.

Jonas nodded and asked Papa if he could have the guitar to take back to Old Brown. To have it destroyed would have been like destroying a child. Papa gave him the guitar the next morning. Jonas returned it. After worship on Sunday he did as Papa had asked.

We never went back to Old Brown. But Jonas had changed. He did his assigned jobs. But he never spoke unless he was spoken to. He stopped writing songs.

In his spare time he stared into space. He never told us what he was thinking. I knew he was trying to figure out how he could manage his life away from us. But what could he do away from the colony? He had no experience out in the world.

At the end of September we took a truckload of frozen geese to Winnipeg to distribute to some supermarkets before Thanksgiving.

I saw that Jonas talked a long time with Hank Reimer, who bought lots of farm stuff from us for his store. He was a Mennonite. He understood us better than most people out in the world because his history was like ours.

That night after supper Jonas told us, "I'm leaving tomorrow for Winnipeg. Hank Reimer offered me a job in his store."

Papa was so surprised that for some time he could say nothing. By then Mama had returned and had heard Jonas's announcement. She started crying and went upstairs. I was told to go to bed too.

But I could hear Papa pleading with Jonas. He tried to convince him that to leave was foolish. Sometimes Papa's voice got loud. But Jonas was always calm.

The next morning after breakfast Jonas shook hands with all the men and told them he was leaving. The women prepared a box of food for him. He kissed Mama and our sisters. Then he picked up his bag and the box of food and walked out of the colony. He hitchhiked to Winnipeg. He was not seventeen yet.

*   *   *

Joshua stopped. The only sound in the room was the ticking of the clock.

"Did you see him after that?" Sara asked, when she realized Joshua had finished.

"Several times a year when we went to Winnipeg, yes. He worked for Hank Reimer that first winter.

Then he got a job in a music store. I remember when I saw him there. He was so happy.

" 'I sell music,' he said. 'I get to play the records and the instruments for people who want to buy. I never knew there was so much wonderful music.' "

"When did he start playing with a group and going on tours?" Sara asked.

"He played with other musicians while he worked in the store. Just around Winnipeg, I think. Sometimes they played in a club. Someone from Toronto heard him one night and offered him a job. So he hitch-hiked there.

"After that we didn't hear from him again until he married your mother. Only then, I think, did Papa finally realize he would never come back."

"Did you write letters much?"

"No. Not much. He was doing well. But to tell us so would be bragging. He did not want to hurt Mama and Papa more.

"He wrote to tell us when he married your mother. And when you were born. And when your mama died. Here. I have the letters in my desk."

Joshua pulled out a small stack of yellowing letters, tied together with a string. "Maybe you would like to read them."

"Oh, yes!" Sara exclaimed softly, taking the precious packet and clutching it to her heart.

"I have talked more than ever before in my life," Joshua confessed. "My throat is hoarse. Enough for tonight. It is late. Tomorrow we can talk more if you want. After you read the letters."

"Thank you," Sara replied, deeply grateful. She

turned and went up the stairs quietly. She didn't want to wake Rebekah and the children.

When she entered the dark room Susannah whispered, "Did you find out what you wanted to know?"

"Yes, oh yes," Sara replied. "Your papa told me everything. He even gave me the letters my father had written him."

"Do you want to read them now?" Susannah asked. "I brought up the flashlight." She handed it over to Sara, then turned her face to the wall. She had fought to stay awake until Sara came back. Now she gladly slept.

16

Sara untied the string from the packet and began sorting the letters. There were scarcely a half dozen. Studying the postmarks, she arranged them from earliest to latest. The first one was exactly twenty years old. The paper was yellow with age. The last letter was not quite a year old. Strange, her father hadn't told her he had written to his people so recently.

Toronto, Ontario
August 2, 1969

Dear Josh,

I got here a week ago. Hitchhiking was slow. Got stranded in one northern Ontario town for four days. Too many people trying to cross Canada using their thumbs. A few are even older than Papa! Some of the young ones are draft dodgers from the States. I was surprised to find so many young men who don't want to be soldiers. Only a few of them come from a tradition of pacifism.

The job looks promising. I'm working in a music store days, and I play with a group at night. Toronto is larger and busier than Winnipeg. So many of the young people I meet seem to be from someplace else. Most of them have deliberately left what they call a "plastic, middle-class life." Some of them had terrible fights with their parents before they left.

I miss all of you. Tell Papa and Mama I love them and am sorry I had to hurt them. Take care.

Your loving brother, Jonas

Sara picked up the next one.

Chicago, Illinois
June 13, 1972

Dear Josh,

So many things have happened during the past three years. I've been touring with a group for two of them.

I got married last week. Her name is Sharon. She's from Denver. She had been studying vocal and instrumental music here in Chicago. Pam, our singer and wife to Chuck from our group, introduced us when we were here on tour a year ago.

Sharon quit her studies to marry me and join our group. I haven't met her folks—but they're giving her a hard time over her decision. She's accomplished on several of the instruments we play. Now we have two good vocalists plus another player. She adds a lot to our group.

Sharon is so good for me. She's teaching me many things about music I never had a chance to learn before.

For me life seems complete now.

Give my love to Mama and Papa and the rest of the family. Best wishes to you on your plan to win Rebekah.

Love, Jonas

Sara studied the snapshot of her parents which accompanied the letter. They were standing beside the bus, their arms around each other, smiling and happy.

She recognized her mother. She was the woman with the long soft hair and the beautiful voice, who appeared frequently in her dreams. Her mother's hair was long and golden, smooth as spun silk. So smooth it looked just ironed.

Windsor, Ontario
February 2, 1974

Dear Uncle Josh,

That's right! Your big brother has become a papa. Sharon had a baby girl last week. We named her Sara Elizabeth. (I hope Mama and Grandmama will be pleased.) She came eight weeks early so is very small. She has to stay in an incubator for several weeks.

When she came early we had to change our tour plans. We planned to be back in Toronto, but the baby didn't give us time. She was born in Detroit, but we had her and Sharon transferred to hospital in Windsor after three days. In Canada we're covered by Ontario Hospitalization. We had no insurance in the States. But living in the colony you probably don't realize how important this is.

Someday I hope to bring my family for a visit so they can see you and you them. Until later, your loving brother, Jonas.

Sara paused to digest the information from this letter before opening the next one. She hadn't known she had spent her first few weeks in an incubator. Nor that she had been born in the United States. And that her mother was an American. Which country was she a citizen of? Or did that make her a citizen of two countries? She'd have to find out.

Toronto, Ontario
August 9, 1976

Dear Josh,
    Thank you for your condolences after Sharon's death. And double thanks for your and Rebekah's offer to take Sara and raise her with your daughter. But I want to try to raise her myself.
    Sharon's absence has created such an emptiness in me. I can't imagine giving up Sara, too. Besides, the group considers her theirs. Pam is like a second mother to her. I think Sharon would have liked that since she and Pam had been like sisters since they were kids. To take Sara from the family she knows might be unfair to her, too.
    Someday when she's old enough to understand, I'd like to bring her to Gnadenhof to meet all of you. Until then, thanks again for your generous offer. With full gratitude, Jonas

Another surprise! Joshua and Rebekah had wanted to raise her with Susannah. Her father hadn't told her that, either. Maybe he was afraid that if she knew, she might want to leave him. *Not a chance that would have happened!* she thought.

Sara tried to imagine what she would have become if raised with Susannah. Maybe then she would have been as satisfied with life here as Susannah was. She thought again of Susannah's statement, "If you never have something, you don't miss not having it." But Sara was glad she had shared life with her father, even if now she had to endure the pain of missing him.

The next letter was a response to Joshua's letter, which must have told of the death of their grandmother, Elizabeth. Her father regretted he'd never get to see his grandmother again, and that she hadn't seen her namesake. Sara was sorry, too. It would have been nice to have known a great-grandmother, especially one whose name she shared.

She took the final letter out of the envelope and read.

Toronto, Ontario
August 24, 1988

Dear Josh,

Now that Sara is old enough for high school, I feel that she should stay put for the school year. There are so many things I want her to learn that we can't teach her on the road. Sciences and lab work, typing and computers. When she's old enough to plan her own life, I want her to have as many choices as possible. I think also that she should be having more time with people her own age.

I'll miss having her with me constantly. She's not very happy with this arrangement either, but I told her that someday we'll have to make a permanent break. So we must practice separating now.

Which brings me to a gloomy and unhappy thought.

Now when I travel without her, there's always a chance something might happen to me.

I've put my modest holdings in her name too. I've also taken out a substantial insurance policy with her as beneficiary. I've made arrangements with a Toronto lawyer to have you appointed her legal guardian in case she ever needs one. He has everything about this in his possession. If anything would happen to me, he would contact you.

If you ever become Sara's guardian, please guide her. Advise her as you think I would.

But enough now of unpleasant thoughts. Next summer I hope to come visit and bring Sara with me. I think she'll be old enough to understand what happened back when I left. And she'll enjoy meeting her relatives. I look forward to meeting your family too. As always, Jonas.

Tears flowed as Sara stared at the letter. So her father had planned to bring her here this summer. Her heart ached. If only it could have happened that way. She hoped he was proud of the way she had behaved in his absence.

She was so proud of him. What Joshua had told her, and what she had read in the letters, showed her he had been even more thoughtful and kind than she had known. Oh, the pain he must have endured in making the choice to leave his people. He had been given a gift, his love for music and his desire to make music. But he had been born into a family and a way of life denying him any expression of this gift.

How torn he must have felt! To be true to his calling, he had to leave his family and tradition. But he had never given them up. She could see his love for them in every word of his letters. How he must have missed them and the life they represented.

She couldn't blame Grandpapa either. He had made a commitment to uphold the traditions and teachings of his forefathers before her father had been born. He couldn't be false to that commitment any more than her father could have been false to the commitment music compelled him to make.

She was proud of her father's calm demeanor when Grandpapa had confronted him. He hadn't made the rift worse than it had to be. His love for his family had continued to burn strong.

From the way they had accepted her, it was clear his family never gave up loving him, either. They had finally come to accept what they couldn't understand or explain. Perhaps this, too, was an example of *Gelassenheit*.

Suddenly Sara realized she was terribly tired. She gathered up the letters and stacked them together neatly. Then she wrapped the string around them and tied it. Quietly she placed the flashlight and the packet on the shelf beside her journal. She lay her head on the pillow and stretched her tired body. Her back ached from sitting up in bed so long. Her eyes burned from reading by flashlight. She couldn't think anymore.

17

The sun was high when Sara awoke. Susannah's bed was made. She had overslept. She dressed quickly and hurried to the kitchen-dining area, wondering how to explain her tardiness. She couldn't understand why Susannah hadn't wakened her when the first bell hadn't.

The women were singing before she entered. Except for Rebekah, who saw her enter, they continued singing.

Rebekah smiled as she came toward her. "Good morning." She kissed Sara's cheek. "Joshua said he keep you up late with his talk and I should let you sleep this morning."

She paused. "I wake up Susannah before the first bell and tell her not to wake you. She is in the tomato field. You can go to her after breakfast."

Rebekah had her arm around Sara's waist as she

propelled her into the dining room. "Sit. I will bring you breakfast." She disappeared into the kitchen.

Sara looked around the now familiar room. That first morning it had looked so strange. Now that it had been her home all summer it felt warm and friendly.

Rebekah returned with a large tray of breakfast and set it before her. It included a tall glass of cold milk. This time Rebekah didn't have to ask whether Sara wanted milk or coffee.

Sara felt a new warmth for her aunt, this woman who had been willing to become her mother. Her heart filled with gratitude for Joshua and Rebekah's willingness to love her as if she were their own.

Sara ate quickly and returned the dishes to the washing area. Rebekah gave her a thankful nod and walked with her to the door. "You go help Susannah and the others now. We will talk again after supper."

Sara walked along the well-trodden lane. She noticed that much of the vegetation had passed its prime —it was preparing for a long winter's sleep. Sumac on the bluffs along the creek were turning red. The lush green grasses along the path had all gone to seed and had turned into a tawny hay. The bean field, where she spent so many hours just a few weeks ago, had been plowed, exposing dark loamy soil.

When she reached the tomato field and saw the many bushel baskets already filled with ripe red tomatoes, she felt a pang of guilt for having slept in. But the smiles of the other women quickly erased the feeling. They didn't look angry. Maybe they knew she had had permission to sleep.

She picked up a basket and went to the row where Susannah was picking. Susannah smiled knowingly and asked, "Everything still all right?"

"Yes, very." Sara began filling her basket.

The two girls worked in silence. Sara sensed that Susannah wondered what she was thinking but was struggling to respect Sara's privacy. Sara appreciated that. She needed to absorb alone what Joshua had told her before she could share it.

Sara didn't have to concentrate on picking tomatoes. Her hands moved automatically while her mind was on the choice she planned to make. She was sure now that she knew what her father wanted her to do. It was what she wanted, too: to return to Toronto and school.

If she had to return to a group home for a time, she would. She could do almost anything, now that she could see a purpose in it. She knew her father had wanted his insurance to pay for her education—at least until she could support herself. Tonight she'd tell Joshua and Rebekah. She wondered what they planned to tell her.

After helping to wash the supper dishes and set the tables for breakfast, Sara and Susannah returned to their room.

Rebekah appeared shortly and said to Susannah, "Papa and I want to talk to Sara. You stay here." Sara picked up the packet of letters to return to Joshua and followed Rebekah.

Joshua was waiting for them. This time Rebekah stayed and sat beside Sara on the settee. For some moments no one spoke. Finally Sara handed the letters to Joshua and said, "Thank you for letting me read these."

Joshua took the letters. "Did they tell you anything you wanted to know?"

"Yes. I think I know what Father would want me to do."

Joshua and Rebekah exchanged looks, then Joshua asked, "And what do you think that is?"

Sara took a deep breath. "I think he would want me to continue my education."

Joshua and Rebekah looked at each other, then both of them nodded. "Yes, we think that, too," Joshua replied.

"I could go back to a group home. After that I could get help and with the insurance. . . ." Sara felt she should offer the alternatives she had thought possible.

"That might not be necessary," Joshua interrupted. "We got a letter from a woman in Toronto who is offering you a home." He handed Sara another letter.

"She is the aunt of that Mennonite boy you met on the bus ride when you came to us," Joshua explained.

Sara took the letter out of its envelope.

1540 Gladstone Road
Toronto, Ontario
August 2, 1989

Dear Mr. Joshua Hofer,

I understand you are the uncle and guardian of Sara Hofer. My nephew Jon Thiessen met her recently on a bus while he was returning to his home in Manitoba. He suggested that she might be returning to Toronto in September and, if so, would be looking for a place to live.

Our only daughter, Joanna, will begin college this autumn. Her room will be available. My husband and I both work. We have been looking for a girl to stay with our two young sons, eight and ten, when we have to be away.

Henry's work often requires that he leave home for several days at a time. I am a nurse and sometimes must work night shifts. If Sara came to us, she could keep the boys company, help with their homework, and generally act as an older sister. The boys are well behaved and independent. They wouldn't cause her problems.

We live near the bus line which goes past the high school Sara attended last year. We wouldn't make demands on her time when she should be in school.

In case you fear sending her to strangers, let me assure you we are Mennonites who feel a natural kinship with Hutterites due to our common heritage. We would respect your wishes concerning her and would do everything in our power to give her a good life.

May we have your response as soon as possible so that we can proceed from here?

In Christian love,
Margot Neufeld

Sara's eyes filled with tears. She could hardly see the words in the last paragraph. But she didn't want to look up and show her tears. Other Mennonites flashed into her memory. They had turned up for her father, and now for her. *Life is full of coincidences*, she thought. *Or is there a greater plan managed by a caring heavenly Father?* Joshua finally broke her reverie.

"Well, what do you think?" he asked.

"I think her offer is wonderful. I want to accept," Sara confidently replied.

Joshua looked at the clock. "Almost eight here. In Toronto it must be almost nine. I will call now." He went to the telephone and dialed.

Margot Neufeld answered on the third ring. She and Joshua talked for several minutes, then Joshua looked at Sara.

"She wants to talk to you," he said, handing her the receiver.

Sara talked to Margot for several minutes. The woman's voice and everything she said pleased her. Sara liked her immediately.

The Neufelds promised to send Sara a plane ticket. She would arrive in Toronto the Thursday before Labor Day. That would let her avoid Labor Day weekend's horrendous traffic. Sara would have time to rest before she had to return to school on Tuesday. She would also be able to shop for new clothes and things she would need for school.

Sara told Joshua and Rebekah all that Margot Neufeld had said. They nodded their approval and remained silent. Finally Rebekah spoke. "Would you like picture of your papa and mama?"

Sara knew Rebekah meant the snapshot which had come in the envelope telling of her parents' marriage. She had yearned to have it but wouldn't have asked.

"Oh yes—if you don't mind parting with it."

"We shouldn't keep pictures anyway," Joshua replied abruptly. He gave the packet to Rebekah, who opened it and looked for the snapshot.

Joshua continued to rummage in the drawer. "Here is something else the lawyer sent after your papa died." He took out a large brown envelope.

"Maybe you should look at it and decide if you want to keep it. If not, we can keep it for you."

Sara opened the envelope. There were only two papers in it. One was a marriage certificate. It recorded that Jonas Hofer, 21, and Sharon Lynn Palmer, 20, were united in marriage on June 2, 1972, in Elkhart, Indiana, by D. J. Kauffman, Mennonite minister.

The other was her birth certificate. It added to her knowledge the name of the hospital and the doctor attending her birth in Wayne County, Michigan.

She put the papers back in the envelope. "I'd like to take them now."

The three adults remained silent until Sara spoke. "If that's all you want to tell me, should I go back to Susannah?"

Joshua and Rebekah looked at each other, then nodded. Sara gave Rebekah a big hug and kissed her cheek. Then she went to Joshua and threw her arms around his neck.

A startled Joshua suddenly became shy. So Sara said, "Thank you for everything." She saw his eyes fill with tears and his tongue could find no words. She turned and hurried upstairs.

Susannah was awake and waiting for Sara to tell her what had happened. Sara's heart was so full she could hardly speak. All she said was, "I'll be leaving a week from Thursday."

"I will miss you," Susannah replied and turned her face to the wall.

18

During the following days Sara anticipated her future. Her heart sang as she worked.

During her quiet hours she wrote letters. In a short one to the Neufelds after the telephone conversation, she wrote how grateful she was for their invitation. "I'm eager to meet you," she added.

Then she wrote to Jon. She thanked him for his letter, for remembering her situation—and for referring her to his aunt. She concluded, "I'm looking forward to seeing you again when you come to visit. I want to tell you all about my summer."

Finally she wrote to her school guidance counselor. She would return in September, she said. Could her homeroom packet and class schedule be sent to the Neufeld address?

Then she wrote short notes to several classmates, telling them her news. She hadn't been particularly close to them. But she wanted them to know she was coming back so they wouldn't act surprised when they saw her. She didn't like being the center of attention and having to explain things before she was ready. Maybe her notes would also tell them she wanted to become better friends.

Not until the third day after the telephone conversation did she fully realize what it would mean to leave Susannah. She looked at Susannah, working intently on the sweater she had started after finishing Mary's pillowcases.

During the past weeks, she and Susannah had grown as close as sisters. Sadness at the thought of leaving Susannah flowed through her. She remembered Susannah's simple "I will miss you." She had yet to tell Susannah this.

Suddenly Sara felt ashamed. She had been so self-centered, thinking only of herself. She hadn't properly thanked Susannah for the precious friendship and trust Susannah had offered when she had come into the community, a stranger.

Sara moved from her bed to sit beside her cousin. Putting her arms around her she said, "I'm going to miss you, too. But I have to go."

Susannah put down her knitting and hugged Sara. The girls sat for several minutes, their arms entwined. Finally Susannah said, "I know. But we must not get too attached to one person. We had the summer. Maybe that is enough."

Sara couldn't decide whether to admire Susannah's calm wisdom or wish Susannah was free to feel more intense feelings.

Susannah broke into Sara's thoughts. "Quiet time is over! We must get back to work."

That evening Rebekah announced, "Grandmama wants Sara to come to her. Susannah is to stay."

Sara followed her aunt, puzzled. She had spoken to her grandmother frequently when they worked at the same task. But they had never been alone. What could she possibly want?

Rebekah read Sara's thoughts. "I think she wants to give you something of your papa," she said simply. "Do not stay long. Gets dark early now."

It took Sara only a few minutes to cross the square and reach her grandmother's house. Grandmama was expecting her. She opened the door as she came up the steps. She motioned Sara to sit on the settee, which was like the one in Rebekah's parlor. The whole house looked much like Rebekah's.

Grandmama did not waste time on small talk. She went straight to the plain, highly polished wood table. She picked up a well-worn beige folder, like those used by students. She handed it to Sara. "This belong to your papa. Look. You might want."

Sara opened the folder. She took out a dozen or more sheets of paper. Different sizes and shapes, they represented the various expressions of a child.

There was a handmade birthday card to "the best Mama a boy could have." The card was elaborately decorated with hand-drawn flowers, perceptively shaded in with colored pencils.

Other sheets had pencil sketches of farm animals. They were hand-drawn from various perspectives, and with unusual sensitivity.

An art course had taught Sara something about the difficulty of drawing lifelike images. In her father's drawings she saw the amazing talent of a child who had never been taught the fundamentals of drawing. She looked at her grandmother, her eyes expressing her admiration.

"Your papa give me the card when he is maybe eight. The other pictures he draw for himself. I save because I think very good."

Sara nodded. Then she spread out several more sheets. They had only writing on them. They seemed to have been crushed. Sara tried to smooth out the wrinkles.

"Some poems, maybe for songs, I think." Grandmama paused. "I find in wastebasket on day after he leave. I save," she confessed. "I never show to Grandpapa. Would make him only sad."

Sara's heart filled with love for her grandmother. Grandmama must have recognized her son's talent. She had probably worried about the conflict it would eventually cause. Had this gift, which had brought her father so much pain and joy, come from his mother? Sara suspected it had. If so, where had Grandmama gotten it?

Suddenly there was the heavy step of a man on the porch. "Grandpapa is home," Grandmama explained abruptly.

Understanding the tone, Sara quickly returned the sheets to the folder before her grandfather entered. But she felt awkward holding the folder.

"So, we have company." Her grandfather's voice was friendly.

"Yes," Grandmama replied. "I ask Sara, to give her things of her papa. That birthday card and some pictures he make."

Grandpapa nodded. "Your papa, he was different." He thought, then shook his head. "We never understood him, but we loved him. We hoped he would come back to us."

The old man's eyes filled. Struggling to control his voice, he said. "We are glad you came."

Realizing her grandparents had nothing more to say, Sara said, "Thank you," and left.

She walked slowly to Joshua's house. The yard lights in the square shone brightly on the grass, dotted with a few yellow leaves already fallen from the trees. The flowers' pristine beauty had given way to brown and drying blossoms. The shrubs showed signs of browning leaves. The air felt crisp, almost frosty. Fall was coming.

The downstairs was empty. The house was silent when Sara entered. She knew the family was in bed, so she tiptoed up the stairs.

Susannah was in bed but awake when her cousin entered. She asked no questions, but Sara knew she was wondering what had happened. "Grandmama had a few papers that had been my father's. She gave them to me," Sara said.

She held up the folder to show Susannah. Then she put it on the shelf with her journal and the brown envelope Joshua had given her several nights before.

She lay awake a long time, pondering the mysteries of life. Questions about her father and his past had puzzled her for years. They had now been answered.

This knowledge of her roots reminded her of a flower's opening. The unknown parts had been like petals, concealed tightly in the darkness of a bud. But this summer's light had opened the bud. What she saw now was beautiful.

19

Sara's last day at Gnadenhof was full of activity. In the morning she worked with the other women as usual. During quiet hour, while she was packing her bag, Susannah handed her a package. When Sara opened it, she saw the sweater Susannah had been working on the past few weeks.

"It's so beautiful!" Sara exclaimed. "I thought you were knitting it for yourself."

"I wanted you to think that." Susannah smiled. "I'm glad you didn't ask any questions about it. I wanted it to be a surprise."

"Well, it is!" Sara exclaimed again. She unbuttoned it and tried it on. "It fits perfectly!"

She looked at herself from all sides and wished for a large mirror, so she could see herself as others would. "But I don't have anything to give you," she added regretfully.

"I have everything I need," Susannah answered.

"Can I send you something from Toronto?"

"Just write many letters," Susannah answered.

"Oh, I will," Sara replied. Then she added, "You're sure your mama and papa won't mind?"

"I think they will want to hear about you, too," Susannah assured her.

Then it was time to go downstairs and outside. There Joshua and Grandpapa were waiting to take her to the airport. But when the girls got outside, Sara saw that most of the adult members of the colony had gathered, waiting to say good-bye.

The women hugged her and told her how much they had appreciated all her help.

Grandmama kissed her cheek and whispered, "You are good. Like your papa." Sara gave her a big hug and thanked her again for the papers.

Each of the men shook her hand. Eli gave her hand a light squeeze.

Sara hugged Elizabeth and Susannah. But she gave Rebekah the biggest hug of all. "Thank you for being my mother this summer."

The look on Rebekah's face told Sara that she had said the right thing. "Come see us again," Rebekah replied as she handed Sara a box of food.

"I will!" Sara promised. Then she looked at the box Rebekah was trying to give her. "I'll be in Toronto in time for supper. And they usually offer food on the plane, too," she said, trying to explain that she wouldn't go hungry.

Rebekah nodded. "Can eat this any time. Mostly cookies. Nobody leaves us without some food."

Sara accepted the box and turned to the group. "Thank you all for *everything*," she shouted. Then she stepped into the station wagon, behind Grandpapa and Joshua. They were already sitting in the front seat, Joshua behind the wheel.

As the car moved away, Sara turned. She waved as long as she could see hands waving back. She had left Gnadenhof. She was returning to the world she had left nine weeks before.

She stared intently out the window, studying the countryside. The last time she had passed this way, it had been night. Now, on this clear and golden afternoon, she could see ripened wheat fields dotted already by harvesting rigs. They looked like ships. They left behind them a rust-colored wake in the vast oceans of waving gold. Purple wildflowers bloomed along the roadside in the tawny grass, under a sky that seemed to stretch blue forever.

The trip to the Winnipeg airport seemed shorter than the trip from the bus station to Gnadenhof. Now Sara was really riding with family. Grandpapa and Joshua didn't talk much to her, but she didn't mind. Their German no longer bothered her. She was even beginning to understand it.

As they approached the airport, the two men became unusually quiet. Sara sensed they felt unsure about what to do next. She pointed out where they should turn into the parking lot. Cautiously maneuvering the station wagon beside the mechanical ticket machine, Joshua gingerly accepted the ticket it spit out.

Sara led the way to the terminal. The men stood

aside while she joined the line waiting for seat assignments. She had only carry-on luggage, she informed the agent. He told her the flight was on time and would be loading shortly from Gate Two.

Sara joined her uncle and grandfather and relayed the information. They escorted her toward the gate. As they approached the X-ray security machine, she told them that only passengers were allowed beyond this point.

Joshua set down Sara's bag and extended his hand. Sara gave him a big hug instead. Then she refused Grandpapa's hand, and much to his surprise, hugged him, too.

"Thank you, again," she said and picked up her bag quickly. She put bag and purse, bulging with the box of cookies, on the belt. Then she went through the arch and picked up her things at the other end. She turned and waved one last time.

She handed her ticket to the flight attendant and boarded the plane. After she stowed her bag in the compartment above her seat, she settled down.

Opening her purse, she took out her comb, mirror, and blush. She lifted her long dark hair out of her collar and removed the rubber band. Then she combed her hair until it hung smooth and loose over her shoulders. She applied a bit of blush.

Just then the plane backed out of the gate. The flight attendants started their routine instructions. Sara fastened her seat belt. She set her watch one hour ahead, leaned back, and sighed. She would be back in Toronto in time for supper.

As she drifted into sleep, she wondered what the

fall would hold. She thought of the Neufelds. And she remembered that warm voice saying, "My name is Jon Thiessen. I'm traveling as far as Steinbach, Manitoba. . . . Who are you and how far are you going?" She had gone a long way. Now the journey continued. She hoped Jon would again be a traveling companion.

The Author

Naomi R. Stucky (formerly Naomi Kejr) was born and reared in Wilson, Kansas. She is the granddaughter of an immigrant Czech Baptist missionary preacher, and daughter of a Baptist minister.

After graduating from Wilson High School, she attended Midwest Bible and Missionary Institute. There she met Solomon Stucky. They married and began a partnership lasting until Sol's death 46 years later.

She was a dedicated wife and mother. During the years Sol was in the ministry, she taught Sunday school classes, organized vacation Bible schools, taught and chaperoned at summer camps, played piano, and sang in the choir.

After Sol's retirement, she helped him with his hobby of Mennonite research and writing, traveling with him to many Mennonite and Hutterite communities.

While assisting Sol, she also reared their children,

and furthered her own formal education and career. She received an A.B. degree and teaching certificate from Western Michigan University in 1954. In 1961 she received an M.A. in teaching modern languages and in 1971, a second M.A. in English. In 1973 she attended MacArthur College, Queens University, in Kingston, Ontario. There she pursued her Type A Ontario teaching certificate.

She taught high school French and English for 31 years. She retired from teaching in 1985.

Stucky has a daughter, Mary, a son, David, and three granddaughters. She is a member of Toronto United Mennonite Church and lives in Brighton, Ontario.